D0013550

09-ARK-952

A WARRIOR'S VOW

"But...I...am your captive," Mia blurted out, stunned at his suggestion. "How can you help me feel less lonely? Why should you care?"

Wolf Hawk badly wanted to reach out and touch her face, which had become flushed. "Just trust that I do care and I will not allow any harm to come your way while you are with me and my people. Did I not feed you well? Are you not in a safe place with comforts all around you? Is not the fire warm against your flesh?"

"Yes, you did all of those things for me, yet...I... am still a captive," Mia said, slowly lowering her eyes. "That word...captive. It fills me with dread."

He reached over and dared to place his hand beneath her chin.

Slowly he lifted it so that her eyes were level with his.

"You are not a true captive," he said.

CASSIE EDWARDS

SAVAGE ABANDON

LEISURE BOOKS NEW YORK CITY

A LEISURE BOOK®

September 2008

Published by

Dorchester Publishing Co., Inc.
200 Madison Avenue
New York, NY 10016

ISBN 10: 0-8439-5878-2
ISBN 13: 978-0-8439-5878-2

The name "Leisure Books" and the stylized "L" with design are trademarks of Dorchester Publishing Co., Inc.

Printed in the United States of America.

10 9 8 7 6 5 4 3 2

Visit us on the web at www.dorchesterpub.com.

With much love and pride,
I am dedicating Savage Abandon
To my son, Brian Edwards.
I also dedicate this book to a very special young lady,
Tiffany Schrock.

Love,
Mom

We stand together, hand in hand,
Holding on to what's left of our land.
Our souls are bound, our hearts entwined,
Who would have thought I'd make you mine.
I know we have something far more,
Than anyone has ever heard of before.
You're my lover, my soul mate,
The very air I breathe.
We'll be together for now,
Through eternity.

By Diane Collett, Poet

WIN A WONDERFUL NECKLACE!

With the publication of *Savage Abandon*, I am giving you, my readers, a chance to win a beautiful Indian necklace made by Eagle Wolf, the Cherokee model who appears on the cover of *Savage Abandon*.

The necklace contains wooden beads that form a circle with three feathers. Two of these symbolize the white woman's family and the red man's family, and the third one in the middle symbolizes the two families coming together. The boning in between symbolizes the many roads that they shall take during their lives.

If you wish to put your name in the drawing for a chance to own this beautiful necklace made by Eagle Wolf's own hands, send your name, address, and phone number to:

Cassie Edwards
6709 North Country Club Road
Mattoon, Il. 61938

The deadline for this drawing is October 31, 2008. I, personally, will notify the winner by phone. Good luck to you all.

Always,
Cassie Edwards

P.S. The winner of the last drawing for the turquoise choker that was offered in *Savage Skies* was a lady from Essex, New York.

Chapter One

Come quickly—as soon as
these blossoms open,
they fall.
This world exists
as a sheen of dew on flowers.

—Izumi Shikibu

Minnesota—1840.
May, Wahbegoone-geezis, *The Moon of the Flowers.*

Spring had awakened across the land, giving rise to the lush blossoms of dogwood and redbud. They gave off no scent, but filled the days with their beauty, as did the forsythia bushes dotting the countryside with their bright yellow flowers.

Bees were busy at work, almost as busy as several small Winnebago girls who giggled and ran through the forest in search of the tiny violets that brightened the forest floor with their lovely purple faces.

When they finally found a huge cluster, they fell to their knees beside them and gently, carefully, plucked several from the earth to take back home to their mothers. The women would enjoy the flowers while doing the daily chores that all

Winnebago mothers carried out each day with love and dedication.

Their hands filled with purple heaven, the girls turned back in the direction of their people's village of one hundred tepees. The village had been established beside the Rush River, near enough for washing and drawing water, yet far enough for safety should the spring rains flood the river over its banks.

Sitting in the midst of the river was an island huddled in mystery. A lazy fog hung low over it at most times, even now making Shadow Island scarcely visible to the girls, who looked occasionally at it, but were not at all afraid of its mystery.

They knew who lived on that island.

Talking Bird.

Like everyone who knew him, they adored the old man.

Talking Bird was the Winnebago people's ancient Shaman, who knew everything about everything.

But rarely did he leave the island.

Those who were in need of his caring touch and kind words were taken to him by canoe.

He was a man who had the skill to cure most ailments.

Rarely had his Bird Clan witnessed him at a loss as to what to do for anything that ailed their people.

The girls ran onward until they came into the village.

Each hurried to her separate home. They were

anxious to give their tiny blessings to their mothers on this most beautiful of mornings.

Not far away, a huge hawk flew above the Rush River, soaring gracefully, peacefully, its bold eyes never missing the movements down below, nor the sounds that came from the island it was circling over.

Despite its watchful, knowing eyes, the hawk could not see through the foggy mist that it was now moving into, not until it was finally on land, standing amid a clearing of willows.

Suddenly a wolf appeared where the hawk had just stood. Powerfully muscled, it bound away into the forest and stopped near a large tepee where smoke spiraled lazily from the hole at the apex of the lodge.

As the wolf ventured onward toward the tepee, it transformed into the powerfully muscled and handsome Winnebago chief known to his people by the name Wolf Hawk. He was a man of twenty-five winters, a chief of well-balanced temper who was not easily provoked.

Clothed only in a breechclout and moccasins, his sleek black hair hanging long past his waist, Wolf Hawk stepped inside the lodge. He stopped there and gazed with love and devotion at his people's Shaman, whom he was proud to claim as his beloved grandfather.

Talking Bird sat huddled beneath a blanket that was wrapped around his shoulders. He was gazing into the lodge fire that had been built in the middle of the tepee.

There was no sound except for the popping and crackling of the fire and some slight wheezing as Wolf Hawk's elderly grandfather clutched his blanket more closely around himself.

He was a wrinkled, shrunken man, but his dark eyes were still brilliant and alive and filled with the wisdom he had gathered during his one hundred winters of life.

Talking Bird was known by all for his wisdom and kindness. He was always interested in the problems of his people. To Wolf Hawk, his grandfather was the best example of what a leader should be.

His grandfather had been like a parent to Wolf Hawk when his father was so deeply immersed in his duties as chief that he could not take time to spend with his son.

Ho, yes, Wolf Hawk and his grandfather had become kindred spirits. Talking Bird had taught Wolf Hawk everything he knew about animals, plants, and what was required of a man.

Awed by his grandfather's vast store of knowledge, Wolf Hawk always loved to sit with him, savoring his words. Wolf Hawk knew he would never forget the insights Talking Bird had shared with him. They were the foundation of his life and would remain with him always.

Talking Bird sensed his grandson's presence. He looked slowly up at Wolf Hawk.

"*Ho*, Grandson," he said, his voice filled with love and respect.

He patted the blankets that were spread before

the fire, then gestured with his bony, long-fingered hand toward Wolf Hawk.

"Come," he said, in his gentle way of speaking. "Sit beside me. Tell me what has brought you to your grandfather's lodge today."

Wolf Hawk knelt and embraced his grandfather, then smiled and sat beside him. "I have not come today for any specific reason," he said in a voice that was rich and deep. "I came only to be with you, and to listen to your wisdom. I must confess to you that I have been restless of late."

For a moment, Talking Bird just gazed quietly at Wolf Hawk. He was proud to claim this man as his grandson. Wolf Hawk was a man of great dignity. He was tall and strong, a warrior loved and admired by all who knew him.

His face was handsomely sculpted. He had midnight dark eyes, and in them was usually an expression of gentle peace. But not today. Today Talking Bird could see the uneasy restlessness that his grandson had mentioned.

The Shaman looked more intently at his grandson. "You have confided in me that you are eager to take a wife, but can find none of the clan's maidens who suit you. Is that what troubles you?"

"No, Grandfather," Wolf Hawk said tightly. "It is more than that. I fear that the peace our people have found here by the Rush River cannot continue undisturbed. We have found such contentment in this refuge, but if white people discover it, I believe they will try to take it from us."

"Whites are always ready to take," Talking Bird

said flatly. "It is a fact that we must always guard against the threat of white eyes."

"Perhaps I have not treated this concern of mine seriously enough. Our people have had no trouble from whites since we moved our homes far from the rest of the Winnebago clans, who continue to be harassed by the white man's government," Wolf Hawk said. "Perhaps I have let our comfortable lives fool me into believing it will be the same forever. But we both know what can happen when the white eyes take advantage of our trust. My father trusted too much and because he did, several of our people died. He and my mother now lie in the ground, because he believed the promises of people with white skin."

"*Ho*, under your father's leadership many died, but we still survive as a clan, my grandson," Talking Bird said thickly. "Just remember that our Earthmaker, our Great Spirit, made us all strong. Each of us has been given his own duties. We both, you and I, have been blessed. Earthmaker placed me in charge of medicine. You have been put in charge of our people, and you have proven yourself worthy of being their leader. We must remember these things, Grandson. Always."

"I always listen well to your wisdom and use it daily," Wolf Hawk said, humbled by his grandfather's knowledge and caring. "Thank you for it."

"Grandson," Talking Bird said. He reached out a hand and gently touched Wolf Hawk's smooth, copper cheek. "You have always found the good in all things and so shall you continue to do. You are admired by those who know you for walking the path of truth and honor."

"Grandfather, you are everything that is good on this earth," Wolf Hawk said as Talking Bird drew his hand back. "I cherish your blessings."

And Wolf Hawk did cherish everything about his grandfather. The old Shaman, whose life had been devoted to the supernatural, had given Wolf Hawk the power to fly as a hawk, and to walk on all fours as a wolf.

Wolf Hawk's people had learned from the death of Wolf Hawk's father that their Winnebago people must depend on things that others did not. They needed mystic power to keep whites away.

Wolf Hawk knew that in his grandfather's younger years, he could also fly as a bird and talk with wolves in his own wolf form, but age had gradually stolen those powers from him.

When Wolf Hawk became chief of their Bird Clan after the death of his father, Talking Bird saw that it was time to share his mystic knowledge with his grandson. He had never done so with his own son, who had disagreed with him over so many things.

Talking Bird had given his grandson the same understanding of the supernatural as Talking Bird had been given by his own grandfather, oh, so long ago.

Wolf Hawk had learned from his grandfather that the spirits, both good and bad, were always at work. Indeed, they controlled the destiny of man.

As Wolf Hawk continued to think deeply, his

grandfather was lost in his own thoughts. He was again admiring this young man whom Talking Bird had successfully shaped into a chief who was honest, just and wise. There was no man, woman or child, who ever doubted his grandson's wisdom.

Ho, his grandson was a man of charisma, and with his rippling muscles and aquiline nose, all women found him handsome.

His grandson would find a woman, and soon. Then his restlessness would disappear and Talking Bird would be happy for his grandson.

"My duties await me, Grandfather," Wolf Hawk said, slowly rising. "*Wa-do*, thank you, for your time and shared wisdom today. I will return again soon to sit and talk with you."

Talking Bird moved slowly to his feet, a bony old hand still holding the blanket in place around his shoulders. He walked outside with Wolf Hawk. They embraced, then Talking Bird smiled as Wolf Hawk transformed himself into a hawk and flew toward his home.

As Wolf Hawk soared over the river, his eyes scanned the land closest to his village.

When he saw nothing awry, he landed some yards from his lodge, where no one could observe him, then transformed himself quickly into his human form.

His long hair fluttered over the straightness of his bare back, and his breechclout flapped with each step he took as he walked into the village.

He stopped and watched his people as they went about their daily activities. He could see peace and happiness in their eyes, and laughed softly when several little girls ran up to him, their dark eyes gazing up into his.

"My chief, we found many violets in the forest today for our mothers," one little girl said, her tiny face flushed with excitement. "They now stand in water in our lodges."

"It is good that you show your mothers your love by taking them flowers to fill your homes with sunshine," Wolf Hawk said. He patted the child who'd spoken to him gently on the top of her head.

Then he suddenly remembered the uneasiness that had been with him of late.

He dropped to his haunches and gathered the children around him. "But always remember that it is not best to wander far from your homes," he cautioned. "Although we have not seen any reason for concern, we must never take our safety for granted. Play amid the circle of our lodges unless you have an adult with you."

He hated seeing the children's smiles turn into wondering frowns, for he did not enjoy bringing doubt into their hearts. But he did know that their world was a dangerous place. He knew that one must never take whites for granted.

They had too often tricked the red man!

"Your fathers and your chief will keep you safe always," he reassured them with a smile. "Now go. Enjoy your games. Soon it will be time to return to your lodges for the noon meal. I smell food cooking even now over your mothers' lodge fires."

Squealing, the girls ran from him, and soon young braves joined them.

Wolf Hawk watched, glad that they seemed to have heeded his warnings, as they all joined together and began playing a game of tag, for none of the children ventured outside the lodge circle.

He stood and gazed with the eyes of a hawk past the tepees, still seeing nothing out of place. Nonetheless, he knew that he must have a meeting with his warriors to warn them of his intuition. Perhaps if there were problems awaiting him and his people, they could still be avoided.

Chapter Two

When in eternal lines to time thou grow'st;
So long as men can breathe or eyes can see,
So long lives this, and this gives life to thee.
                    —William Shakespeare

Water splashed like sparkling crystal in the wake of the scow as it worked its way up the Rush River, toward St. Louis.

Mia Collins stood on the deck with her father and the man hired to help row the scow. She was eighteen years of age, petite, with long auburn hair, and she was wearing a comfortable full-length cotton dress.

She stood back away from the men so that she wouldn't be in the way of the long oars that moved the scow through the river.

She was enjoying the warmth of the sunshine on her pretty round face as her luminous green eyes took in the sights along the riverbank.

She loved to see the occasional deer dipping its nose into the water for a refreshing drink, or a mother opossum carrying its babies on its back.

She loved to smell the scent of the wildflowers that dotted the land, as well as the cedar aroma coming from the towering trees that intermingled with oaks and elms in the shadowy forest.

She and her mother and father had waited to wander once again along the river in their scow, until the warmer weather of spring. Her father had longed for this journey all winter when he felt cooped up either at home, or working on the ships that he helped build for a huge company in St. Louis.

But this spring, the trip downriver was not the same as before. After traveling some distance in the scow, her father had said they must turn back.

He had confided in his wife and daughter about pains that he'd been feeling in his chest. He feared a heart attack was imminent.

They had turned the scow back in the direction of St. Louis, where their home had been locked up until their return. They were in the habit of spending the later months of the summer there when it got too hot to live on the scow.

Mia looked slowly around her now, at the bargelike conveyance on which her family had lived during these past weeks. It was built of logs, lashed together to provide a deck where a little cabin had been built. Here they could take shelter if there were storms and here their provisions were stored away from the elements.

They traveled by day and spent the nights beside a campfire near the river, while her father's assistant boatman slept aboard the scow, which was tied up near them at the embankment.

If they did leave the scow to sleep on land, on the coldest of evenings, when they needed the warmth of a campfire, they slept huddled in separate blankets beside the fire.

Mia gazed over her shoulder at a small longboat that skipped along in the water behind the scow, tied to it by a sturdy rope. It was there in case a quick escape was needed, for the larger vessel was not easily maneuvered.

Out of love and pride, Mia's father had painted her name on both sides of the longboat.

With concern, she gazed at her father. His name was Harry. He was over six feet tall, yet seemed shorter now because he stood stooped over as though the world lay heavy on his broad shoulders.

He no longer had thick, red hair, but instead gray.

He had the same luminous green eyes as Mia, but they were filled with terrible sadness since the death of his wife.

Mia blinked back tears as she thought of how her mother had died. It had been on a day as beautiful as this one, and the scow had been leisurely making its way between tall cliffs along the river.

Mia had looked up just in time to see a lone Indian fitting his bowstring with an arrow. The flight of the arrow had been swift and deadly.

But it seemed the man had wished to kill only one person. After he had watched Mia's mother fall, an arrow implanted in her chest, he had fled and had never been seen again.

Mia would never forget that moment. Her mother had died instantly, and the shock of seeing her struck down had caused Harry Collins to suffer a minor heart attack.

It had been up to Mia to take over. She had grabbed hold of her father's oar, and along with the assistant boatman, had rowed the scow to dry land on the far shore.

Her father had recovered from his attack enough to say a final good-bye to his wife, his sweet Glenna, after the assistant boatman had dug a grave for her beneath a blossoming apple tree, her mother's favorite of all trees. Mia would always remember the beautiful blossoms that had perfumed the air above her mother's grave with their hauntingly sweet scent.

It was the very next day that they continued homeward, the loss of Mia's mother lying heavy on everyone's hearts except for the man who was assisting Mia's father to row the scow.

Mia looked at him now as he stood on the side of the boat opposite her father.

His name was Tiny Brown.

He was a small, boisterous man, his sun-bronzed face speckled with freckles, his brilliant red hair brushing his shoulders.

He was an admitted card shark, and although he was skilled at helping with the scow, he persisted in annoying and teasing Mia, showing her one trick and then another with his cards.

Mia was glad that Tiny had never openly flirted with her, and she knew why that was so. He didn't dare try anything with her under the protective eye of her father.

Mia shuddered even now as she watched Tiny cast her a mischievous glance over his shoulder and nod to the deck of cards in his right shirt pocket.

She knew that he was anxious to show her another trick, although she was tired of everything he said, or did.

All of her troubled thoughts were swept away when Mia's beautiful yellow canary began warbling, perhaps in response to some yellow finches that were darting here and there close to the scow, singing their own sweet songs.

Mia went to the spot where she kept the cage secured just inside the shade of the shed.

She leaned down and gazed directly into her bird's black eyes.

"Did you hear the finches, Georgina?" she asked in a soft, melodious tone. "You sweet thing. I have never heard you sing any more beautifully than you are singing this morning."

She heard a soft mocking laugh and glanced quickly over at Tiny.

She stiffened when she saw that he had stopped to stare at her bird, then at her.

She knew that he despised her canary. He complained all the time about the "racket" it made.

His dislike of the canary had proved to Mia just what sort of man he was. Anyone who couldn't love something as sweet as her tiny canary surely didn't have a good bone in his body!

Feeling uneasy in the presence of this man, Mia moved closer to her father.

She glanced at Tiny again, then looked into her father's sad eyes. "Papa, I don't mean to make any more trouble for you, but I just can't feel comfortable with the likes of that man on our scow," she murmured. "Papa, please consider finding someone else at the next town? Please? I just don't trust this man. And I don't understand how you can."

"He has done us no harm," her father said. "And you know how hard it is to find help these days, especially someone who don't mind bein' away from family on these long river journeys."

He paused, cleared his throat, then said, "Anyway, we truly don't have much longer before we'll be home. Can't you ignore him for the few weeks it will take us to get there?"

"It seems so long, Papa, before we'll arrive home," Mia said, swallowing hard.

"But it truly isn't," Harry said. He glanced over his shoulder, at the tiny weasel of a man.

Then he gazed into Mia's soft green eyes. He raised a hand and gently drew his long, lean fingers through her waist-length auburn hair. "Be patient?" he said, giving her the smile she adored. "For me, Mia? For me?"

"Papa, usually when you give me that smile, I can't say no to you, but this is different. I just can't stand that man," Mia said, visibly shuddering. "Please reconsider. Surely someone will be eager to take Tiny's place for the amount of money you are paying for assistance."

Harry placed a hand on her soft, round cheek. He gazed intently into her eyes. "If it means that much to you, honey, yes, I guess I'll do what you suggest, but it might delay our trip for several days," he said. "It ain't that easy, you know, to get reliable help."

"Yes, I know," Mia murmured. "Tiny Brown is proof enough of that."

Tiny's ears had picked up the whole argument and he knew now that he would be out of a job before long. He resented Mia's interference with every fiber of his being.

It was hard for him to find jobs.

Anywhere.

He seemed to rankle everyone's nerves almost from the very day he was hired to do this or that!

Well, this time he was not going to be let go so easily. He was going to show this miss prissy a thing or two before being given the boot.

He eyed the canary that she was so proud of.

His eyes lit up with a sudden idea.

By jove, he would use that canary to get back at Mia!

He would wait for just the right opportunity to open the door to the cage and watch the bird fly to its freedom.

Yep, he was going to make Mia pay for treating him as though he was beneath her. No one treated Tiny Brown like that and got away with it.

Mia grew cold inside when she saw Tiny glaring at her lovely bird, and then giving her a slow sort of knowing glance.

She was afraid that he had something on his mind now besides cards. But surely she was wrong.

He might be a man she despised, but she could not believe he would take his spite out on her lovely Georgina.

She went back and sat in the shade of the shed beside the birdcage. Georgina hopped closer to her and began singing again, this time even more beautifully than before.

"Oh, Georgina, what would I do without you?" Mia whispered.

Yes, ever since her mama's death, she had found a measure of peace listening to the canary's sweet song. She just wished the little bird had the same effect on her father.

She glanced at him now and saw how lost and alone he seemed without his wife.

She worried about the shortness of breath and chest pain he was so prone to having.

She was afraid that one of these days he would have a massive heart attack, and then she would be all alone in the world except for her canary.

She looked heavenward and said a soft prayer that she hoped would get her through these difficult times, praying especially to have the strength not to worry so much.

She gazed out upon the loveliness of the land the scow was gliding past.

Then she thought of that Indian who'd stood on that bluff, with his bow and arrow and hate in his heart for whites.

She knew that where there was one Indian, there were surely more, yet she had not seen hide nor hair of any others since that one warrior had taken her mother's life.

"Mia, bring me my pipe and tobacco," her father suddenly said, drawing her attention back to him.

"Yes, Papa," she murmured, scurrying to do something that she knew would make him feel better, at least for the moment. He loved his pipe sometimes more than food.

She took his pipe and bag of tobacco to him and watched him prepare the pipe, then leisurely smoke it.

"Ain't cha going to share that with me?" Tiny said, laughing sarcastically.

Harry frowned at Tiny. "Not on your life," he growled out. "Not on your life."

Another shiver passed through Mia, for she felt certain that Tiny was up to no good. This sarcasm seemed to signal a change of attitude, for he never did anything to openly aggravate her father. He had tried not to get on her father's bad side.

It seemed he knew that he wouldn't be a part of their lives for much longer.

She wondered just how much Tiny *had* heard when she'd been discussing him with her father.

Chapter Three

What we behold is censored by our eyes,
Where both deliberate, the love is slight.
Whoever loved, that loved not at first sight?
  —Christopher Marlowe

The birdsongs in the trees had stilled. Even the breeze seemed to hold its breath as two whiskered men, dressed in denim breeches and faded plaid shirts, slunk through the forest.

Each carried a rifle, and their squinting eyes searched avidly for the traps they had placed there earlier in the day.

It was very rare for them to forget where they had set their traps, but this time, they had decided to go far beyond their usual trapping lines, and they had become disoriented in the unfamiliar territory.

They had left their horses tethered close to a stream where there was thick grass for them to feast upon, not worrying about being able to locate them.

Not until now, anyway. They were lost, and frighteningly enough, were now concerned about not only being unable to find their horses, but where they had left the many pelts they had gathered up today. They had hidden them at an old fort they had found upon their first arrival in this unfamiliar territory.

What worried them the most was the realization that they had traveled into Winnebago country. They had always known an Indian village existed somewhere in this forest, but until today had made certain to avoid it.

"I don't like it one bit," Jeb growled out. "You should've listened to me, Clint. We had no business temptin' fate like this by comin' so close to an Indian village, or traveling so far from the fort. Good Lord, Clint, we were doin' well enough stayin' away from this part of the forest. I wish now that we hadn't taken such a risk. I say let's leave this place right here and now. To hell with the remaining traps. A few more pelts ain't worth the sweat it's causin' us. I smell like a skunk. That alone might lead Injuns to us."

"Oh, jist shut up and bite off a plug of yore chawin' tobaccy and take your nervousness out on it instead of me," Clint snapped back. "We ain't seen hide nor hair of an Injun. It's my belief they stay close to home 'cause of bein' scared of the soldiers and bein' chased down and taken to a reservation. So jist shut up your whinin', Jeb, and keep yore eyes peeled for those traps. They cain't be all that far from here and I ain't leavin' 'em behind, especially if some frisky red fox got hung up in one of 'em. Those furs are worth the chance we're takin'."

Jeb frowned at Clint, but did as he suggested. He grabbed a wad of chewing tobacco from his front shirt pocket and placed it in the right corner of his mouth. At first he nervously sucked on it, then began earnestly chewing it.

He spat a long string of rust-colored spittle from his mouth, wiping it from his lips with the back of a hairy hand. "No matter what you say, I don't like this situation we're in one bit," Jeb growled. "I'm goin' back, Clint. I'm gonna find my horse and that fort and gather up my portion of the skins and I'm leavin' this dang place. You can stay if you want to gamble with gettin' caught and havin' your scalp hang on one of those Injun's scalp poles."

"I ain't never seen a scalp pole, so I doubt there ever was such a thing. I'm not sweatin' about losin' my hair to any Injun," Clint said. He chuckled as he reached up and ran his fingers through his filthy, tangled brown hair. "Anyhow, no Injun could want a scalp bad enough to take mine. The way it's been itchin' these past few days, I'd swear there's fleas in it from those animals we've caught."

Jeb stopped quickly.

He held a hand out in front of Clint.

"Stop," he said, his eyes wide as he stared at something straight ahead of him. "Lord Jesus Almighty. I jest found two of the traps, Clint. Look yonder. Seems we caught way more than a fox in 'em."

Clint almost vomited when he looked and saw what Jeb was staring at. "No," he gasped, turning pale at the sight of two young braves lying on the ground, their ankles caught in separate traps, blood pooling on the ground beneath them.

"They ain't movin', Clint," Jeb said hoarsely. "And my Lord, look at the god-awful blood beneath them on the ground."

Clint swallowed hard. "The traps must've cut right through a major vein," he said. "They didn't have a chance in hell of escapin' the steel jaws of death."

"You know what that means, don't 'cha?" Jeb said, his voice dry with shock and fear.

"Yep, it means we better get the hell outta here if we want to live another day on this earth," Clint replied, yet he took another step closer. He hadn't ever seen an Indian up this close.

He just had to take a good look. The two braves were no doubt full-blood Winnebago. Their hair was coal black and waist long. Their copper skin was smooth and hairless, very different from Jeb and Clint's, whose faces were covered beneath their long beards. ·

The young men's chests were also hairless, making Clint wonder if they shaved all the hair off their bodies every day. They wore breechclouts and moccasins, but otherwise they were naked.

"Whatcha doin?" Jeb gasped out. "Come on, Clint. This ain't the time to fool around. We've gotta put many miles between us and those two Injuns. We truly might be scalped if their people realize we're responsible for their deaths." He squinted as he looked more closely at their faces. "They ain't all that old, you know. Look at 'em. I bet they ain't no more than fourteen years old."

Jeb then glanced at the knives sheathed at the

braves' waists, and at quivers of arrows on their backs. Two bows lay on the ground beside the youths. "Betcha they were out hunting," he said thickly. "They never thought they'd end up bein' the hunted."

"None of this was done on purpose, so don't say such a thing," Clint said, nervously looking over his shoulder. "It's time to go, Jeb. Now."

"Damn it all to hell," Jeb grumbled. "We should've been more careful where we placed our traps. We knew we were gettin' way too close to an Injun village, but just couldn't resist. We saw too many fat beavers and fox in this particular area not to take some for ourselves."

"Jeb, why cain't you listen to reason?" Clint whined. "The only thing I can think of now is gettin' the hell outta here. Let's go!"

Jeb's eyes were still transfixed on the lifeless Indians. He realized he felt nothing at the sight of their bloody bodies. To him, they were not much different from the animals they caught in their traps every day.

The only difference was that he and Clint couldn't sell 'em and make money from the kill.

"You've got that look I know so well. What would you do . . . empty the traps and place them somewheres else to catch a fox or beaver in 'em?" Clint growled out. "Have you gone nuts on me, or what? Come on. We've got to get outta here, and fast."

Jeb laughed throatily. "What do you think I am? Looney?" he said. He stepped farther away from the fallen braves. "I know the importance of gettin' away from this place. We've got enough pelts hidden at the old fort. I say let's leave the entire area now, then come back later and get our pelts after the Indians have cooled down. And don't forget that the savages surely have more on their minds than the loss of two young braves. They have the survival of the entire village to concentrate on. It's a fact that all Injuns have to watch their backs, because the United States government is rounding up as many as possible to send away to reservations."

He smiled smugly. "Yep, the Injun tribe these young ones belong to won't want to cause a stink over the loss of just two braves when they have their entire tribe's survival to worry about," he said.

"I say we forget everything but escapin'," Clint said. "No matter what you think, they'll be out for our hides, Jeb. As soon as they discover these bodies, they won't stop until they find us. I say we hurry down to the river, and wait for the opportunity to steal a boat. You know how busy the river is these days, with so many folks goin' to St. Louis to do business there. We'll go as far as St. Louis, too. We'll meet with the men who buy our pelts, and tell them about the rich hides that we'll be bringing to them as soon as we can."

"But . . . our . . . horses."

"You've got to accept that we've lost 'em somewheres in this damnable forest," Clint said sourly. "We've lost our way. I ain't even sure we can find the river quick enough so that the Injuns won't find us and hang us."

With only their rifles in their hands, they started running from the gory scene. Then Jeb stopped and turned to look again at the dead braves.

"Whatcha think you're doin'?" Clint growled out. "Come on. We don't have time to mess around."

Jeb ignored him.

He ran back to the fallen braves.

He knelt, reached out and yanked an amulet necklace from around one of their necks.

He chuckled as he placed the fancy, beaded thong around his own neck.

"Put it back," Clint said as he came up and slapped Jeb across the back of his head. "Take it off. Throw the thing away if you ain't going to put it back around the Injun's neck again. It can only bring us trouble . . . bad luck."

Jeb turned and glared at Clint. "Don'tcha ever hit me again, or you'll not live to regret it," he snarled.

"Your threats don't frighten me, Jeb. Now do as I say. Put that amulet back on that Injun, or throw it away," Clint demanded, his eyes glaring angrily into Jeb's.

"Stupid, I'm keepin' it," Jeb said, putting a hand protectively over the amulet to keep Clint from grabbing it from him. "Don'tcha know, amulets are worn for good luck."

"Stupid, did you see the good luck it brought the savage that wore it today?" Clint asked, laughing sarcastically. "He's dead, Jeb. Damn dead."

Jeb ignored Clint.

He started running again, and Clint soon caught up with him.

They ran and ran, until they were both too breathless to take another step, and then they saw the river up ahead through a break in the trees.

"See?" Jeb said, smiling at Clint. "The amulet's already brought us good luck. We found the river."

"Yep, but we lost two horses and maybe a stack of pelts, too, and I call that bad luck, Jeb," Clint said breathlessly. All the same, he was relieved to see the shine of water up ahead.

They would go and hide by the river until night fell; then they would travel alongside the river until they found a moored boat that had tied up for the night, so that its occupants could get some sleep on shore.

When the travelers awakened the next morning, their boat would be gone and so would Jeb and Clint. They would be out of range of the Indians' hatred and need for vengeance!

They looked over their shoulders to make sure they weren't being followed, then loped onward until they found a thick stand of bushes where they could hide.

Chapter Four

———

Futile the winds
To a heart in port—
Done with the compass,
Done with the chart!

—Emily Dickinson

Another day closer to St. Louis, Mia was just about to go rest in the shed when she saw her father grab at his chest and grow pale.

As he gasped, he dropped the oar on the deck and his pipe fell from his mouth and bounced into the water, sinking slowly into the dark abyss.

Her heart pounding with fear for her father, Mia rushed to his side and began helping him down on the deck of the scow.

"Papa, what is it?" Mia cried, struggling with his weight even though he was a thin man.

"If it ain't one thing, it's another," Harry gasped as he leaned his full weight against Mia.

Seeing that Tiny Brown offered no help, but instead just stared straight ahead as he continued manning the scow, Mia gave him a dark frown, then helped her father onto the cushion of blankets that were always there, used as his bed at night, or for an occasional rest during the day.

"What do you mean?" Mia said, concentrating only on her father now.

She would give Tiny a piece of her mind later.

She only hoped they could find someone else to board the scow as her father's assistant in the next town they came to.

"It's this heart trouble that I've been having," Harry said, glad to be stretched out on the blankets so that he no longer had to put his entire weight on his daughter. She was so tiny, she looked as though she might blow away in the breeze.

He glared at Tiny whose back was to them, finding him more and more loathsome as each day passed. The little man had not even offered Mia a helping hand when she needed it the most.

"Papa, do you think this attack was worse than the others?" Mia asked, on her knees now beside her father. She dipped a cloth down into the river, then wrung it out just before placing it on her father's sweat-beaded brow.

"Might've been. I don't know," Harry said. He closed his eyes and rested as she continued bathing his brow. "It only lasted for a moment."

"You'd best not do any more work today," Mia said, laying the damp cloth aside.

She eyed the oar that her father had abandoned when he felt the discomfort in his chest.

The scow, which was propelled by two wide oars called "sweeps," was designed to be rowed by two men.

But Mia wasn't a man. Still, she knew that if they

were going to get to shore, where they could put in for the night, she must take up one of the oars.

Until now, the scow had floated effortlessly, even lazily, along the Rush River, which would eventually run into the Mississippi and finally take them home, to St. Louis.

Mia knew that helping Tiny get the scow to shore would be grueling work for her. She wished that her parents had never decided to travel so far from their home this time. Instead of enjoyment, this trip had brought them nothing but disaster and sadness.

"Papa, you just lie there and rest," Mia said.

For her papa's sake, she had to try to appear comfortable with the task that lay ahead of her. Her father's health came before any discomfort she might feel while helping to row the scow to shore.

She stood up, sucked in a nervous breath, then stooped over and picked up the oar.

"Mia, what on earth do you think you're doin'?" Harry blurted out as he struggled to get to his feet.

But his recent attack had drained his energy, and with each effort he made to try to get up, his heart went wild inside his chest.

He realized that he had no choice but to rest and allow his daughter to do the work of a man, something he had vowed never to let happen!

"Papa, I've watched you often enough to know how this is done," Mia said, lowering the oar into the water.

She ignored Tiny when he turned around and gawked at her, then gave her a cynical, mocking laugh.

"Just you shut up," Mia said, still working the oar although each stroke made her arms feel as though they were going to fall off. "Help me head this thing toward shore, Tiny. We're stopping for the night."

Her eyes widened when just as they floated around a bend in the river, she saw the old abandoned fort that sat a short distance from the banks of the Rush River. She had seen this fort many times before as they had made their yearly trek down the river.

"Look!" she cried. "It's the old fort. You can tell that it's abandoned. Tiny, help me get there. We'll set up camp at the fort for the night."

Suddenly Georgina burst into song, sending her lovely melody into the air.

Mia looked over her shoulder at her canary, smiled at her sweetness, then continued working hard to pull the oar through the water.

"That damn bird and its screeching noise," Tiny growled as he helped head the scow toward land. "I don't know why you keep that aggravating thing on board this scow. It ain't a proper place for you to have a bird, and I wish you wouldn't force me to listen to its nonsense."

"You aren't the sort of man who would enjoy the lovely music that my canary serenades us all with," Mia said, frowning at Tiny. "She is a piece of heaven on earth. But someone like you doesn't recognize goodness when you see it. You're too full of spiteful meanness."

She glanced down at her father, who had fallen asleep, then frowned at Tiny again. "As soon as we reach the next town, you're history, Tiny," she said smugly. "We'll find someone who'll be willing to help us get back to St. Louis without constant griping. It's a city of opportunity. Everyone wants to experience it."

"Oh, jist shut up," Tiny growled out. "You'll never be able to replace me, so just relax and enjoy my company."

Mia visibly shuddered. She was so worn out and dispirited, and his spiteful tongue wasn't helping one iota.

She was beginning to feel that they would never reach St. Louis while her father was still alive. It seemed so far away now that her father was ill.

She glanced down at him again. She felt tears burning at the corners of her eyes as she saw just how weak he suddenly seemed to be. She was afraid that he might die if she couldn't get him some help, but she had no idea how far they were from the next town along the Rush River.

For now, finding a good resting place seemed the most important thing to do.

He was so pale.

And his breathing seemed so shallow.

Perhaps if she could get him on dry land, away from the constant rocking of the scow, he might be able to get enough rest that on the morrow he would feel as good as new.

But in her heart of hearts she doubted that. She had never seen him this sick before.

Now she had only Tiny to depend on. Thank heavens he had made no sexual overtures toward her, for had he done that, her father would have taken his last ounce of energy and shot Tiny, leaving them truly alone on the river.

But now that her father was so ill, Mia couldn't help fearing for her safety. She planned to keep an eye on Tiny's each and every movement once they settled down for the night on dry land.

Her thoughts were interrupted when she felt the bottom of the river with the tip of her oar. They were close enough now for Tiny to jump off and pull the scow to shore, as her father had always done before he began having these spells. Tiny had been doing it now for the past week.

She looked over her shoulder at her father when the scow was finally secured against the embankment. Tiny had just finished tying up to a sturdy tree.

Her father was sound asleep. She hated to disturb him.

But she knew that he would be better off once he was on dry land and away from the constant movement of the scow. He would rest much more comfortably.

And she was sure that rest was the most important thing now for her father. She just wished she knew how far they were from a doctor.

She would not rest until she heard a physician say that her father wasn't in any immediate danger, that all he needed was plenty of rest, that which he had not had since the journey back to St. Louis had begun.

She knelt down beside her father and eyed the abandoned fort, then looked over at Tiny. "Tiny, I think it's best that you go and investigate the fort before we help Father there," she said. "I don't see any sign of life, but we should just make sure."

"Probably only a coon or two makin' their home there," Tiny said over his shoulder as he began walking toward the fort.

He laughed throatily and went onward, soon disappearing behind the dilapidated walls.

"What's going on?" Harry asked, awakening with a start. He was so used to the constant movement of the scow, that when it was stopped, he knew it even in his sleep. "Where are we?"

"Papa, we're tied up now," Mia murmured. She placed a gentle hand on his cheek and cringed at its cold wetness, the sort of perspiration that came only when one was ill.

"Tiny is inspecting the old fort that we've seen before," she said. "We've got to make sure no one else is living there, although I doubt anyone is. I see no smoke, which means no one has a fire made to prepare food, and I hear no sounds coming from that direction."

At that moment, Georgina suddenly broke into song again, breaking the stillness of only moments ago.

Mia looked quickly at her bird, for the first time

wishing she would be quiet. She wanted to be able to hear if someone was living at the fort, or making camp nearby.

Mia knew that Indians lived somewhere along this stretch of the river, and she had no wish to encounter them.

She hadn't caught sight of any Indians since she had seen the one who took her mother's life with his bow and arrow. Since then she had seen only deer and other forest animals through the brush and trees.

"Coast is clear!" Tiny shouted as he reappeared at the open gate of the fort. He waved his arms and hands toward Mia. "Come on. See for yourself."

"Shush up, Tiny," Mia said, her spine stiffening as she realized that his voice was echoing throughout the trees that surrounded the fort, carrying to God only knew whose ears!

Tiny frowned at her, then returned to the scow. "You can tell that some animals have frequented the place, but there are several cabins for us to choose from for our night's stay," he said, already gathering supplies from the shed. "I'd say the larger one would be best for us. I imagine that's where the big shots made their residence. It seems to be in the best shape."

"Tiny, be sure to gather up all of the blankets and go and make a pallet for Father first," Mia said, holding her father's hand as he moved slowly to a sitting position. "Then come back for him. I shall gather together what I believe we'll need for the night. Is there a place inside the fort where I can warm up the food that Mother canned for us before we started on this year's trip?"

"There ain't only a fireplace but also a small pot-bellied cooking stove," Tiny said. He bent on his knees before Harry.

He then swung one of Harry's arms around his neck. Struggling and groaning, he helped Mia's father to his feet.

"Tiny, what are you doing?" Mia gasped, turning pale at her father's weakness. "I told you to go and prepare my father a place to lie before taking him to the fort."

"And who made you my boss?" Tiny said, glaring at Mia. "You drop what you're doin' and go ahead of me and you make the pallet. We'll come back to the scow together later to get the supplies we'll need for this one night."

Sighing heavily, knowing now what a battle she was going to have without her father's authority to control this tiny, loud-mouthed man, Mia dropped what she was doing and grabbed several blankets. She ran on ahead of Tiny.

When she got inside the walls of the fort, she stopped and looked slowly around her.

Though people had obviously lived there at one time, it was long ago by the looks of things. The fort seemed eerily quiet now, as though ghosts were there, eyeing her.

She counted ten cabins in all, but only one of them still had a roof, and that was the one Tiny was walking into now, helping her father along beside him.

"This one, Mia," Tiny said over his shoulder. "Come on. Hurry. Spread out the blankets. Your father ain't no lightweight, you know."

Mia ran past him, and when she got inside, she again stopped and looked around her. It was cold and damp, and in disrepair.

Cobwebs clung from one side of the room to the other.

She shivered when she saw the remains of some animal, only its bones lying there.

"Well?" Tiny said, impatiently waiting for her to spread the blankets. "We ain't got all day, you know. I'd like to get a fire going and get our stuff in here with us before night falls. Who knows what or who might come upon us and . . ."

"That's enough, Tiny," Harry growled out. He found the strength to yank himself away from Tiny. He went slowly over to Mia and reached for the blankets. "Here, darlin'. Let me help you."

"Papa, are you feeling better?" she asked, eyeing him hopefully. "You do have some of your color back. And you seem to be able to stand there without assistance, whereas earlier, I . . ."

"Just you quit frettin' over this ol' man, do you hear?" Harry said, bending over enough to drop the blankets to the floor. "But I do think I'll let you spread out the blankets for me and make me a soft bed for the night."

Mia did this quickly, then placed a gentle hand

on his arm as he slowly sank down onto the blankets, sighed heavily and closed his eyes.

"I just need a wink of sleep, that's all," Harry said. He opened his eyes for long enough to smile up at Mia. "Better go and get Georgina. She ain't used to being away from you for long. You're like two peas in a pod. You've hardly ever been separated since your mama purchased her for you."

"Yes, I'd best go and get her," Mia said, scrambling to her feet. She looked over at Tiny. "Then I'll fetch the rest of the things. You just go and gather wood and get a fire going in both the fireplace and the stove. I'd like to prepare something warm for Papa tonight."

Tiny glared at her and brushed past her as he went outside.

As she stepped from the cabin, she saw him hurry out through the wide, open gate of the fort. She followed him, but she headed toward the scow while he turned toward the darker depths of the forest where he would gather wood.

"I wouldn't put it past him to just run away and find someone else's company for his trip to St. Louis," she whispered to herself as she ran to the scow.

Yes, it would be just like him to leave them stranded, but she hoped and prayed that he wouldn't, even though she despised him with every fiber of her being!

"We'll be alright, won't we, Georgina?" she said as she stepped aboard the scow, where her tiny yellow bird was springing from one of its perches to the other, its eyes never leaving her.

Mia hurriedly gathered up what she felt she would need for the night, placed everything in a travel bag, then swung it from the scow to dry land, and slung it over her shoulder.

Then she turned and grabbed up the cage by its handle and took it to the cabin, setting it on the far side of the room from the spot where her father lay, so that when Georgina began singing she wouldn't wake him up.

Mia paused long enough to look at her father again, something inside her telling her that he might be worse than he had tried to claim. He rarely dropped off to sleep this early in the evening. And he still seemed to be breathing shallowly.

All of these things made her feel terribly anxious, for she knew that if anything happened to her father, she would find it hard to make it in this lonely world with only her bird as a companion.

She turned with a start at the sound of footsteps entering the cabin, breathing a sigh of relief when she found that Tiny had returned. He brought with him an armload of wood.

She truly had never thought the sight of him would be welcome to her, but she had to admit to herself that he was a lifeline of sorts now that her father was disabled.

"I'll get a fire goin' in no time flat," Tiny said, dropping the wood to the floor in front of the fireplace. He laughed to himself when the sudden noise and movement made Mia's bird flap frantically around in her cage.

"You frightened her," Mia said, hurrying to Georgina's rescue. She picked the cage up and brought it close to her face. "Sweetie, calm down. Nothing is going to happen to you. Not while I'm here to protect you."

Mia's soothing voice calmed the bird, but across the room, stacking wood in the fireplace, Tiny gave the bird an evil glare over his shoulder.

He could hardly wait to open the door of that cage and watch the bird fly out of it.

He could hardly wait to see Mia's face when she saw that it was gone.

These thoughts made his work seem effortless as he got a huge fire going in the fireplace, and then also in the potbellied stove.

"Ready for the cook here," Tiny said, stepping aside so that Mia could get started with the evening meal, which would be made from the canned goods she had brought into the cabin.

He just wasn't ready to go hunting for meat tonight.

He'd take this time to relax and wait for just the right moment to make this pretty little thing's world turn upside down. He was going to release her bird as soon as Mia was fast asleep tonight.

"I wonder what's in those other cabins out there?" he asked idly, sitting on a rickety chair that stood beside a faded old oak table. He shrugged. "Probably nothin' worth lookin' at, or takin'."

Mia stirred the tomato soup.

The tantalizing aroma awakened Mia's father.

He sat up, then lay back down when he felt an unaccustomed dizziness.

He didn't complain to Mia about it. She had enough worries on those pretty, tiny shoulders of hers.

Mia was aware of mosquitoes buzzing around in the room. She eyed her father. If he got malaria from mosquito bites, that would be the last of him.

She stepped away from the stove and went looking inside the wooden cabinets that lined half of one wall opposite the fireplace.

She smiled when she found some folded mosquito netting. No doubt mosquitoes were always a problem there beside the river.

She unfolded the netting and stretched it over her father, even covering his head, securing it so that he had enough room between his face and the netting to breathe.

She wondered if she should awaken him for supper?

But yes, she knew that she should. Her father would not want to pass up an opportunity to eat his wife's home cooking!

She went back to the stove and continued stirring the soup, the delicious aroma from it now spiraling slowly into the air. She was eager to eat, too, for the soup was a dear reminder of her mother.

She glanced at Tiny, who sat a few feet away on

the floor before the fire in the fireplace, playing cards with a pretend partner.

She stiffened when she heard the distant baying of a wolf. Suddenly she felt very, very vulnerable!

Chapter Five

One word is too often profound
For me to profane it,
One feeling too falsely disdained
For thee to disdain it.
                    —Percy Bysshe Shelley

Wolf Hawk had just returned home from the se-
cluded spot where he always went to speak his
private early evening prayers, when he heard a
woman's voice outside his tepee.

He recognized the voice.

It was Dancing Fire, the mother of twin braves
who were the age of thirteen winters.

Wolf Hawk was always ready to open his home
and heart to Dancing Fire, for she had been widowed not so long ago. Her husband, Short Bow,
had died in the river when his canoe capsized
during a storm.

Wolf Hawk sensed that something was not
right with Dancing Fire, for there was distress in
her voice when she spoke his name.

Normally she had the soft voice of fresh, new
breezes that came to this land in early spring.

She was as dear and sweet as those winds, and
when he realized that something was causing her
distress, he always did what he could to ease it.

He hurried to his entrance flap and shoved it aside. He looked out on a woman of beauty, yet one whose face was lined now with wrinkles that had appeared after she'd lost her true love in the river.

In her dark eyes was a renewal of that distress.

"What is it?" Wolf Hawk asked, searching her eyes. "Why do you come to me with such worry, not only in your voice, but also your eyes?"

"My sons," Dancing Fire said, nervously wringing her hands. "Neither has returned from their hunt. They have been gone for far too long now. I fear something bad has happened to them. Oh, Wolf Hawk, were I to lose them, too . . ."

"Do not think such a thing," Wolf Hawk said, gently interrupting her. He reached out and took her hands in his in an effort to calm her. "You said they left to hunt. How long ago?"

"Early this morning," Dancing Fire murmured, lowering her eyes in shame that she had waited so long to come to her chief for help.

But she had not wanted to embarrass her sons should they appear only moments later in their lodge.

"They took no provisions with them," she blurted out as she looked quickly up at Wolf Hawk. "They wanted to prove they could care for themselves without carrying provisions from home to ensure their comfort. It was just another way to prove to their mother that they were brave like their father. They are brave, but there are so many things that could harm them while they are away from the safety of our village."

She swallowed hard, then said, "My chief, they are so young," she said softly. "They long to walk in the moccasins of a warrior when they are, in truth, only young braves."

"You should not lose trust in the abilities that were taught them by their father. They know how to survive away from the safety of their lodge and people," Wolf Hawk said. He lowered his hands from hers. "They probably were enjoying their hunt so much that they decided not to return home as soon as they had initially planned. I am certain you are just allowing a mother's fears to consume you needlessly. The young braves will surely arrive home anytime now."

"Although I know that you are speaking what you think is truth, in my heart I feel a strange disconnection, as though my sons no longer have breath to connect them to me," Dancing Fire said, tears filling her eyes. "Please listen to what my heart is telling me. Go find them and guide them back to safety."

Only now, as she persisted in asking him to do something he had already said was probably not needed, did Wolf Hawk understand the depth of her fear. Usually, when he spoke comforting words to a mother, she accepted them and went back to her home and sometime later discovered that he was right, and she was wrong.

But this time he saw that he might be the one

who was wrong. He could not take the chance that the two braves might be in trouble.

"Say no more," Wolf Hawk replied. He reached for her and drew her into his gentle, comforting embrace. "I will gather together several warriors and we will go and find your sons. We will tell them how they have worried their mother. We will bring them home to you. Soon."

She clung to him. Sobs wracked her body. "Thank you, my chief," she cried. "Oh, *wa-do*, thank you. You must find them. They must be safe. They are all that I have left in this world."

"No, you are wrong about that," Chief Wolf Hawk said. He stepped back a little so that he could look down into her eyes. "You have your chief and all of your Bird Clan, who are of your extended family. We are all as one. If you are afraid, so is every one of our people afraid. If you laugh, we all follow you in laughter. Today when we bring your sons home to you, we will all celebrate their safe return with you. Remember this, Dancing Fire. You are never, never alone."

"*Ho*, yes, I do know that," Dancing Fire murmured. She swallowed hard. "It is just that my lodge is so empty without my family to fill it with love and laughter. I have lost one voice, my husband's. I cannot lose two more."

"You go to your home and do your beadwork while I gather warriors to find Eagle Bear and Little Bull," he said.

He stroked his fingers through her long black hair. "Time passes quickly," he softly encouraged.

"Soon you will be embracing your sons. It will be up to you whether or not to scold them for staying away longer than is usual from the safety of their village."

"I will forbid them to hunt for several days," Dancing Fire said. She wiped fresh tears from her eyes. "But they love the hunt so much, as did their father."

"And that is why you always have fresh meat on your table, just as you will today when they return from their hunt successful," he said, drawing his hand away. "They are the sons of their father, are they not? Did he not always bring meat home for his family? Your sons are taking his place so that you will be proud."

"I am so very proud already," Dancing Fire said, then straightened her back and tightened her jaw. "I shall do as you say. I have much work awaiting me in my lodge. I have two pairs of moccasins to bead for my sons, as well as vests to complete for them."

"Then go in good spirit and sit by your fire and do your beading," Wolf Hawk said. He patted her shoulder again. "Go now. I will return home soon with your sons."

"May our Earthmaker be with you," Dancing Fire said, then swung around and walked away from Wolf Hawk, her long, beaded dress swaying as her full hips moved beautifully with each step.

Wolf Hawk admired her, not only for her courage, but for her beauty. He hoped that one day a warrior of her age would step forward and offer her a horse as a bride price.

She needed a man in her life again.

It was not good to center her entire world around sons, for they would soon take wives, which would leave Dancing Fire totally alone in her lodge.

But it would be hard for her to find a husband, just as it would be hard for her sons to find women they could marry, for they could not marry within their own clan, and the other clans were far from their village. Many had already been confined to the horrors of reservation life.

Even he had begun to be concerned about how he might find a woman he could offer a bride price to. He did not want to chance leaving his people for the amount of time it would take to find another Winnebago clan, and he certainly did not dare go anywhere near a reservation to find a woman.

That might lead the white soldiers back to where he had made a safe haven for his people.

For now, for today, he would place his duties to his people, to this mother, ahead of the hungers of the flesh that had begun to plague him.

Perhaps he would never marry. That thought brought a strange ache at the pit of his stomach, for he hungered to have a woman to share his bed and his life.

He wanted sons!

Putting his own needs from his mind, and centering his thoughts on the matter at hand, Wolf

Hawk went from lodge to lodge until he had enough warriors to ride with him.

As they rode through the fresh, new grass of spring, enjoying the scent of apple blossoms wafting through the air, Wolf Hawk and his warriors kept an eye out for any movement in the forest.

First they saw a deer feasting on grass, and then a fox meandering through the brush, confident that the red men with bows and arrows were not there for his hide.

Soon after came a female fox with her small kits, scrambling to catch up with the father.

Although fox fur was one of the most desirable of all for winter hats and clothes, today the animals were not pursued.

Wolf Hawk had been touched by the sight of the tiny kits, their fur not yet as red as their parents'. Their innocent play and ignorance of danger made him wish he did not have to kill in order to have warmth and food, but that was the way it was. That was the circle of life.

And he had to make certain that his people lived their own circle of life with enough food and pelts to make their lives comfortable. Always he feared that white people would come and take it all away from them.

He thought of the white eyes he had seen on the river in their many types of vessels. Thus far, none of them had stopped or become a threat to his people.

They all seemed to have a faraway destination

in mind and he always wondered where it might be, and what was calling them there?

He shrugged and centered his full attention again on the search. He and his warriors had now traveled quite a distance, much farther than the usual hunting grounds of the young braves.

They had been taught that to go farther was to tempt fate. And he was beginning to wonder if that was exactly what those two braves had done. If not, why had Wolf Hawk and his warriors not found them yet?

Suddenly his horse neighed nervously and shook its mane. Wolf Hawk saw something up ahead beneath a tall old oak that made him gasp in horror.

He heard the same gasp all around him and knew that his warriors had also seen the scene of death that broke Wolf Hawk's heart.

He and his warriors had found the young braves, and the news that they must take back to their mother would destroy her, for her sons were both caught in a white hunter's claws of steel.

They lay in a pool of their own blood, blood that had come from the wounds on their ankles, where the trap had severed the skin and arteries.

"They could not have died instantly," one of the warriors said as he sidled his horse next to Wolf Hawk's.

"*Ho*, it is evident that they slowly bled to death, for they could not free themselves of the white man's traps," Wolf Hawk said, his voice tight with emotion.

He knew what must be done, but he hated the thought of taking the fallen sons back to their mother. Still worse would be telling her of the horrible way they had died.

That was something no mother should have to be told.

Wolf Hawk rode somberly onward until he came close to the fallen youths. He dismounted and knelt beside them.

He bowed his head and said a silent prayer, then looked slowly around for any sign of who might have caused the deaths.

Of course, he knew that it was the work of whites. But where were they?

Had they come to see what they had done? Had they fled the wrath of the Winnebago, which they must have known would fall on them?

He saw the youths' bows nearby their bodies. Their quivers were still on their backs.

But he saw no game. Apparently they had caught none before they had stepped into the jaws of death.

The poor boys must have lain there, afraid and filled with pain, as death slowly consumed them.

Then he noticed something that made his insides tighten. Little Bull's hunting amulet was gone from his neck, yet his brother's was still in place. The white hunters who had set the traps must have come upon the dead youths.

Fearing that their own lives would be forfeit once the bodies were discovered, they had fled, leaving the two young braves lying in their own blood. But apparently before they left, one of those hunters had yanked the amulet from around Little Bull's neck.

Wolf Hawk now knew that whoever wore that amulet carried the proof of his guilt in taking two young lives.

"Help me free them from the traps," Wolf Hawk said tightly. He felt an urgent need to start tracking down the killers. But that had to wait.

A mother was waiting for the delivery of her sons and he would not assign that duty to anyone else. He had promised her that he would bring them home to her.

He had just never imagined it would be in this way.

He'd truly thought he would find them, scold them, then send them home to their mother and let her decide what their punishment should be for having caused her such distress. Now that distress would be unending.

Once the boys were freed of the traps, blankets were taken from the bags of two warriors and wrapped gently around the bodies.

Wolf Hawk carried one of the bundles to his horse and carefully draped it over the back of his steed, while one of his warriors did the same with the other.

"With great sorrow in our hearts we must take the young braves home to their mother," Wolf Hawk said, mounting his horse, a black stallion with a white star design painted on each side of its body.

Slowly they turned back in the direction of their village.

Filled with a need for vengeance such as he had never felt before, Wolf Hawk headed for home, followed by his warriors.

Wolf Hawk dreaded to be the one to carry such terrible news back to a mother who adored her sons.

But he was the chief of his Bird Clan. He must fulfill his duties to his people, even this most painful one.

Dancing Fire would be totally alone in the world now, except for her Winnebago people who would always embrace her with their love. But despite his reassurances earlier, Wolf Hawk knew that that sort of love just would not be enough today.

He anticipated Dancing Fire's remorse, for he felt it, too, as though these two young braves were of his own flesh and blood . . . his sons. He felt the same about all of the young braves of his village.

Chapter Six

Her dreams in the bright day
Make the suns evaporate
And me laugh, cry and laugh,
Speak when I have nothing to say.
                                        —Samuel Beckett

All was quiet at the fort except for an owl that sat on the roof of the cabin where Mia and her father now slept. Tiny sat watching them as a slow fire burned in the fireplace.

The owl's hoot-hooting set Tiny's nerves on edge, as though he sensed the creature's strange song so early in the evening was an omen of some kind. It was indeed a haunting sound, causing goose bumps to rise on Tiny's flesh.

But nothing was going to dissuade him from what he had planned. Exhausted, Mia and her father had fallen asleep before it was fully dark, and that suited him fine. He had a task that required secrecy.

With a cold, wicked gleam in his eyes, where the fire's glow reflected like the flames of hell, Tiny turned his gaze to the covered cage sitting on the table.

Georgina, Tiny thought smugly to himself.

Yep, he had plans for that sonofagun songbird

whose happy warbling would soon be silenced. He would never again have to watch Mia pamper it with pieces of apple or any kind of fruit that she found in the forest.

"You'll have to find your own tidbits, little bird," Tiny whispered, only loudly enough for the bird to hear.

Yes, he had mapped out a plan to take his vengeance against a young woman who rankled his nerves and who insulted him anytime she liked because he was the hired help, and beneath her.

He did not see why she had any right to behave so grand, when she was just the daughter of parents who enjoyed spending part of the year on water instead of in their home on dry land.

Yep, despite Mia's pretty, innocent smile, she was nothing but a river rat.

Yep, he'd take her down a notch or two when she found the birdcage empty on the morrow.

Of course, she would know who'd opened the door of the cage, but that didn't matter none to him. He knew his days were numbered under the employ of Mia's father.

So be it.

So were her bird's!

He reached for the cage, which was covered by a soft cloth that Mia carried with her only for that purpose. As Mia prepared herself for the night, she also prepared her beloved canary. She felt it deserved privacy as it slept, as did she.

Careful not to shake the cage as he lifted it from the table, which might cause the bird to squawk a warning to Mia, Tiny dared not even breathe as he tiptoed his way to the door. He had purposely opened it after he knew that Mia and her father were sound asleep.

Yep, he had mapped out a plan, and by jove, he would succeed. He could hardly wait to see Mia's expression when she found the empty cage.

The bird was always the first to get her attention in the mornings. She would remove the cloth and feed the canary, then smile as the bird began its warbling.

To Tiny, the dratted singing seemed to go on forever. He would be happy never to hear that bird again. He would prefer Mia's anger at him when she found the bird gone over the constant noise the creature made.

He had so often wanted to snatch that thing from its cage and wring its neck!

But this plan seemed better.

The bird would surely die quickly out in the wild. Perhaps, even, a hawk might sweep down from the sky at daybreak and eat the bird as its breakfast!

That thought brought a wicked grin to his whiskered face.

He tiptoed out of the cabin and took the bird cage beyond the open gate of the fort. When he reached the darkening shadows of the trees that sat back from the river, he set the cage on the ground, then chuckled as he opened the door and waited for the bird to fly out of it.

But the bird just continued to sit on its perch, eyeing Tiny with its small, black eyes. It looked at him so trustingly, Tiny could not help feeling a quick pang of guilt.

"You sonofagun, stop lookin' at me like that," Tiny said. He picked the cage up and shook it, hoping to loosen the bird from its perch.

But the canary clung to the perch with its tiny claws, its eyes still peering directly into Tiny's. Tiny set the cage on the ground again.

"Well, seems I'm going to have to give you some help," Tiny grumbled.

He reached his hand inside the cage, only to get a finger nipped by the bird's sharp beak.

"Ouch!" Tiny exclaimed, rattling the cage as he yanked his hand free. He sucked on his sore finger.

His eyes narrowed angrily as he again bent low and gazed directly into the bird's eyes. Then without wasting any more time, he quickly reached inside the cage and grabbed the bird. He drew his hand out, opened it, then watched the canary fly upward and perch on a limb just above Tiny's head.

Suddenly he saw a tiny white glob of something falling away from the bird. Tiny knew what it was, but couldn't get out of the way before it landed on the very tip of his nose.

"Lord a'mighty," he groaned, swiping the mess from his nose. He doubled a fist and held it up in the air, waving it at Georgina. "You stupid bird. Fly. Scat. Get outta here. And if you drop one more mess on me, I'll grab you and kill you. I'm tired of messing with you. Do you hear? Fly! Fly!"

Suddenly Georgina took wing and flew away. With the canary's disappearance, Tiny was overwhelmed by guilt.

He knew that the bird wasn't used to being free to fly. More than likely it would be so disoriented, it would fly right into a tree and fall to the ground, easy prey for any animal that might happen along.

"What am I doing?" Tiny said, running his fingers through his whiskers. "Worrying about that bird?"

He shook his head, then grabbed up the cage and hurried back inside the cabin. He put the cover on and waited for morning and Mia's reaction.

As he stared down at Mia sleeping there so innocently and trustingly, he could not help feeling guilty for depriving her of something that meant so much to her.

"But she deserves this, for the way she has treated me," Tiny whispered, trying to justify what he had done.

"Yep, you'll soon see that you cain't push people like me around. If you do, you'll live to regret it," he said, yawning as the lack of sleep closed in on him.

He smiled toward the covered cage, then stretched out on a blanket in front of the fireplace and soon fell into an uneasy sleep, with dreams of the canary coming toward him, twice its normal size, its claws widespread and ready to attack him.

He awakened with a start. Sweat was beading up on his brow.

He went to the door and slowly opened it, then gazed outside to see if the bird had returned. When he saw nothing, not even any sign of the owl, he went back and sat down before the fire.

This time, he stayed awake. He wasn't ready for more nightmares about giant canaries!

Chapter Seven

Money of th' earth brings harms and fears,
Men reckon what it did, and meant,
But trepidation of the sphere
Tho greater far, is innocent.

—*John Donne*

As shadows lengthened all around them, Wolf Hawk and his warriors rode into their village bearing the dead bodies of the two youths, their futures snuffed out long before their prime.

A huge fire was burning in the center of the village. It was built each evening in preparation for the lengthy night ahead, when animals prowled and the fire was necessary to keep them out of the village.

The fire's glow fell upon the face of Dancing Fire as she stepped out of her lodge at the sound of horses approaching the village.

Wolf Hawk saw the sudden horror in her eyes when she spotted her sons hanging, lifeless, across the backs of the horses.

Their stillness, the way they were placed on the two steeds, the blood that had spread onto the blankets wrapped around them, was proof that her worries had been confirmed.

Dancing Fire ran toward the approaching warriors. Her arms were outstretched before her, her hands visibly trembling, as she began wailing and crying her sons' names. The rest of the village people came from their lodges, joining her mourning when they saw what had caused Dancing Fire's horrible distress.

Wolf Hawk felt a terrible ache in his heart at the loss of two such promising braves, who would have one day become proud warriors to help protect their clan. He drew rein where Dancing Fire now stood, her face wet with tears that would not stop until she could cry no longer.

"Why?" Dancing Fire cried as she pleaded with Wolf Hawk with her bloodshot eyes. "Where . . . did . . . you find them?" She shuddered as she gazed from one son to the other. "There is so much blood."

"I will explain, but first let us get your sons laid out for all to mourn over," Wolf Hawk said.

He truly hated having to spread the word of exactly how these brave young men had so needlessly died.

All knew of such traps, which could capture more than animals. But none of his people had ever been hurt by one before. White trappers had never ventured so near their village in the past.

But now Wolf Hawk realized his intuition had been right. He had felt an uneasiness that he'd shared with his grandfather, a fear that white people would begin to intrude on Winnebago territory. He was beginning to understand why those feelings had come to him on this day.

He wished only that he had paid more heed to what his heart had told him and searched the forest. If so, he might have found the white trappers. He might even have stopped their evil before the two braves' lives had been snuffed out.

Well, he would find the culprits now. They would pay for their crimes! He would not rest until it was so.

Lovingly, the fallen youths were taken from the horses and placed upon pelts near the central fire. Their eyes were peacefully closed as though their spirits hovered near.

Their mother knelt between the two boys, a hand on each as Wolf Hawk stood tall over them. He slowly turned and gazed at his people before speaking.

Tears shone in all of their eyes. A look of horror was captured on their faces. Fear as well as the pain of having lost two of their young ones had captured their souls.

They all stood quiet as they awaited their chief's words.

"Wolf Hawk, how . . . ?" Dancing Fire asked, her voice filled with emotion. "Please . . . tell . . . me. Tell me now."

"Your sons died in the white man's steel traps," he said as he gazed down directly into her eyes.

He saw the horror of his words register in them, and knew that she understood too well how her children had died.

Slowly.

Painfully.

Striped Arrow, a warrior with much honor among Wolf Hawk's people, who had been standing solemnly beside his wife, his own son on his other side, stepped up before Wolf Hawk.

"White trappers are in our forest?" he demanded. "We must find the evil ones and stop them," he said. He slid his hand down, to rest upon the knife sheathed at his right side. "Now, my chief. Now!"

"It will be done," Wolf Hawk said. He turned again to gaze lovingly, yet sorrowfully, into Dancing Fire's eyes. "Their deaths will be avenged."

"We are a peaceful people," Dancing Fire said as she returned his gaze steadily even though her heart was breaking at today's losses.

"Our peace has been disturbed, two lives have been taken. We must make certain it does not happen again," Wolf Hawk said. He gently placed a hand on Dancing Fire's shoulder. "While you mourn your sons, a search will begin for the evil white men."

He stepped away from her and turned to look from one warrior to the other. "Before night falls completely upon us with its darkness, we must go and search for those who have brought grief into our people's hearts today," he said tightly. "Separate into three groups. Each ride in a different direction. Carry your rifles. I want to bring the culprits in alive if we find them. We will decide the way they will die, later."

They all nodded, then ran to their horses and rode from the village.

Those who rode with Wolf Hawk fanned out through the forest to begin their search. Their eyes scanned in all directions for movement or any signs of the trappers.

After riding for a while, Wolf Hawk saw something a short distance from his horse that filled his heart with keen, passionate anger. He had found several traps filled with dead animals.

When he saw movement in one of the traps, his anger escalated, for this animal had not died yet, although its fur was matted against its body with blood. It was evident the creature was suffering terribly.

The animal, a beautiful red fox, sensed the nearness of the warriors and turned its head to look directly into Wolf Hawk's dark eyes. For a moment, Wolf Hawk and the fox became as one, and Wolf Hawk could feel all its pain.

Wolf Hawk did not hesitate.

He leapt from his horse. He bent low over the animal, then grabbed his knife from its sheath.

Again, he looked directly into the animal's eyes. "My friend, I will end your suffering," he said, then did what he had to do, although thrusting the knife into the beautiful animal made him heartsick.

Ho, yes, he had taken the lives of many animals during the hunt. But he had never left any behind to suffer. His aim had always been accurate.

He turned and gazed up at his warriors, who were still on their horses, gazing down at him.

"Search diligently, my warriors, for any more animals that might be suffering like this one," he said thickly. "Do as you must if you find any. Then gather up all the dead animals and bag them; also gather up all the traps you find. Make a travois to transport the traps. Take them to our village. Leave them near my lodge. I will destroy them so no one can ever use them again."

They traveled onward, searching for more traps, but found none.

They did come upon something else, however . . . two abandoned horses.

"Two horses mean there are two men," Wolf Hawk said, dismounting.

The horses were tethered beside a small stream where they could drink and where there was tall, fresh green grass for them to eat.

It was strange to Wolf Hawk that the trappers who owned these beautiful steeds could treat them so well but never stop to think about the suffering they brought other animals.

He stroked the brown mare first, and then the strawberry roan, as he looked from one horse to the other.

There were saddlebags on each.

He looked into one of them and saw clothing, some provisions, and a flask that had water in it.

It was obvious that these two horses had been left behind while those who owned them had fled the area on foot, no doubt after the discovery of the two dead braves.

He could envision the evil ones' fear, even taste it, upon finding that they had caught more than animals in their traps. They had killed two boys and they knew that those boys had homes, and families who would seek to avenge their deaths.

"These horses belonged to the trappers," Wolf Hawk said, stroking a thick mane. "But what puzzles me is why they would leave them behind? Where will they go without them?"

"Perhaps they will return for them," one of his warriors said, edging closer to the strawberry roan.

He reached out and stroked its withers. "This is a fine steed," he said. "It is muscular. It is beautiful. It is well fed and healthy. How could anyone abandon it?"

"Fear causes many misjudgments," Wolf Hawk said. "The white men are running from their misdeeds. They must realize that the wrath of the Winnebago people will come down hard on them if they are found."

"But why not flee on their horses?" another warrior asked. "Would not it be faster?"

"When you are filled with fear like these men must be feeling, logic is not a pure thing inside the heart and mind," Wolf Hawk said bluntly. "They must have run instinctively upon their discovery. They are probably still running. Perhaps they were afraid to take the time to return for their horses. That is all I can make of their decision to abandon them."

"It may be they will still return for them," another warrior said.

"They forgot not only their horses in their haste to escape what they had done," Wolf Hawk said as he stepped away from the animals. "They forgot that our people are fine trackers. I am one of the best. My warriors, all of you return home with the pelts and traps and these two horses, which are now ours. I shall search for the tracks of these two men. If I find their tracks, I will follow and discover where they have gone."

He grabbed his horse's reins and quickly mounted. "My warriors, when you arrive home with the traps and the pelts, leave the traps just outside my lodge," he commanded. "Remove the pelts from the animals that have been found in the traps and give both the meat and the pelts to the mother of the two fallen youths."

Each warrior gave a nod, then continued collecting the pelts, while others made a travois for the traps. When this was all done, the warriors all turned their steeds in the direction of their homes and rode away.

Wolf Hawk rode back where he and his warriors had found the dead boys, and when he arrived there he leapt from his steed.

He held the reins as he looked for the tracks that had been made by the trappers, and when he found those leading away from the traps, he led his horse behind him as he walked slowly alongside the tracks. To his disappointment, they soon led him to the river. There they stopped. But he saw no white men anywhere.

He fell to a knee beside the river, examining the tracks more closely.

He was confused as to how the trail could go as far as the river and then disappear, for the men had arrived in Indian country on horses, not boats.

"Where could they have gone?" he whispered to himself, angry at this turn of events.

He hated to think that those men might never be found and made to pay for their crimes. But they seemed to have sprouted wings, as Wolf Hawk did in his hawk form, for how else could white men just disappear into thin air?

He gazed at the darkness that now lay thick around him. The moon became visible as clouds slid away from it.

Darkness had fallen so quickly, it seemed as though a dark cloak now clung to Wolf Hawk.

He hated the fact that he would have to return home and tell the mother of the fallen youths that their murderer had gotten away and would surely never be found.

That meant vengeance might never be achieved for Eagle Bear and Little Bull!

Disgruntled, Wolf Hawk mounted his steed and rode back in the direction of his home.

He knew where he must go. Back to Shadow Island, to seek advice from Talking Bird, who held wisdom concerning all things.

Wolf Hawk just couldn't believe that he would

never find the trappers. He must! He could not give up.

Surely the trappers would return to hunt again. The rich furs that could be had in this forest were too tempting to ignore.

Ho, they would surely feel that it was safe again later and would make the mistake of returning to the land where they had spilled Winnebago blood.

Chapter Eight

I am coming, I come,
By meadow and stile and wood.
Oh, lighten into my eyes and heart,
Into my heart and my blood!
                    —Alfred, Lord Tennyson

The moon lit a huge hawk as it soared over the Rush River, soon disappearing among the wolf willows on Shadow Island.

The transformation was quick, and Wolf Hawk then sprinted, on foot, to Talking Bird's lodge. He stopped just outside the entrance flap to again think through the events of the day and his role in them.

This was the first time he felt a weakness in himself, for two young braves had died needlessly under his leadership. Wolf Hawk felt as though he should have been able to avoid such tragedy if he had listened more closely to the warnings of his intuition.

He looked heavenward and spread his arms up and out toward the dark sky. "Earthmaker above, how did this happen under my leadership?" he whispered, believing that his sorrowful, troubled words, would reach the stars.

Then he lowered his arms to his sides, turned

and faced the closed flap, and softly spoke Talking Bird's name.

"Come," Talking Bird said, his words reaching through the buckskin fabric of the flap.

Wolf Hawk held the flap aside and stepped inside, where his grandfather was again sitting beside his lodge fire, a blanket wrapped around his bent old shoulders.

Talking Bird looked up at Wolf Hawk. "I heard the wings of the hawk above my lodge as you came through the wolf willows," he said. "I knew that you would soon be here. It is late, my grandson. What brings you to your grandfather with such concern in your eyes?"

He gestured with a hand toward Wolf Hawk. "Come and sit beside me," he said thickly. "Tell your grandfather everything as you have done since you were a child. It is my pleasure to listen and offer you comfort."

Wolf Hawk sat down beside Talking Bird. "Grandfather, when I was here before, talking things over with you, do you recall my telling you about an uneasiness that I was feeling?" he began, looking into the dark depths of his grandfather's eyes.

"*Ho*, I recall your concerns," Talking Bird said, nodding. "I thought I gave you comfort with my words. Tell me why you are still so troubled. Why do you come again so soon?"

"I come to tell you that I have wronged my people, especially the mother of two fallen sons," Wolf Hawk said, slowly moving his eyes to the fire. His memories of seeing those two young braves caught in the traps were almost too hard to bear.

"Tell me more," Talking Bird said. He reached from beneath his blanket and placed a comforting hand on his grandson's bare knee. "Talk and your pain shall be lifted from your heart. I will take the pain into my own if it will help dispell the guilt that I hear heavy in your words. You speak of two fallen sons. How were they downed? By whom?"

"Dancing Fire, a woman of much strength and courage, who not long ago lost her husband in the thrashing waves of the river during a sudden storm, has lost now not only her husband, but also her sons," Wolf Hawk said, finding those words so hard to say, and even harder to bear. "Eagle Bear and Little Bull. They did not return home as they usually did after a day of hunting small game. Their mother came to me with much concern in her heart. I took many warriors into the forest and began a search for them. It took us much farther from our village than the young braves were allowed to travel. They disobeyed their elders, and they found more than game. They found the traps of white hunters. When they stepped into the traps, they could not escape them. Their life's blood left their bodies through the wounds on their ankles. My warriors and I found them lying in their own blood, their eyes locked in death stares."

Wolf Hawk rarely heard his old Shaman grandfather gasp in horror, but he did now.

He looked quickly up at Talking Bird, seeing tears flowing from his old eyes.

"You feel it, too, the same as I," Wolf Hawk said, lowering his eyes. "Such a heavy heart I feel. Such loss!"

"It is not for you to feel the guilt that I know you are carrying within your heart," Talking Bird finally said. He again gently patted his grandson on the knee. "What you have told me is news that eats away at my very soul, and yours, but it is done and you must move on to the next day and be prepared for whatever else the Earthmaker above has for you. Sadness or happiness. It comes as it is given to you. Today sadness came and it shall stay for a while among our people. Even after the youths are prepared for burial and placed in the ground with final prayers said over them, there will be sadness. But you must look forward to better times. You cannot change what has already happened. But you can prepare for what might happen next, be it good, or bad. Only the Earthmaker knows."

"I feel such guilt for having allowed this to happen," Wolf Hawk said, swallowing hard. "I do feel that I should have done more than I did to ensure the safety of our children."

"You said that the two braves wandered farther than where they were taught to venture?" Talking Bird said, searching Wolf Hawk's tearful eyes.

"*Ho*, that is so," Wolf Hawk said, slowly nodding.

"Then the fault lies not on your shoulders, but instead on the shoulders of those who did not obey the rules of our people," Talking Bird went on, again patting Wolf Hawk on his knee. "*Ho*, I mourn for the deaths, but I also know that the braves brought their own deaths on themselves by not obeying rules they were taught from the moment they knew how to talk and walk."

"But I had feelings of uneasiness," Wolf Hawk said tightly. "Had I . . ."

"Do not speak with such guilt in your heart," Talking Bird said, interrupting him. "You cannot be with all of the young braves at all times to see that they follow the rules laid down for them. You cannot follow every hint of danger that you feel. You have made a good home for your people on this piece of land. Until today, it has not been spoiled by the white man's greed. You have seen that our people live in a peaceful setting beside the river. For now, this piece of land is ours.

"You have made wise rules for our people to live by. If some youths do not follow those rules, you are not to blame."

"My guilt has been eased by your guidance and kind words, but it is now my place to find the ones who *are* guilty—the trappers," Wolf Hawk said firmly. "But there is always the fear of bringing trouble into our people's lives if the white government discovers that we have taken vengeance."

"A man has the right to go on the warpath if one of his people has been wrongfully killed," Talking

Bird said as he drew his hand back beneath his blanket. "I know that the need for vengeance is strong inside your heart. Do what you must, and I tell you now that no white man will stand in your way. I will make it so, my grandson. I will make it so."

"I followed the tracks of the two hunters, which led me to the river. There they stopped," Wolf Hawk said, sighing. "And, earlier, I found horses tied up by a stream. These trappers did not come to our land by boat, so how could they disappear at the river if they did not have a boat to carry them away?"

"Whites can be clever," Talking Bird said, his voice drawn. "But I know they cannot wave a hand in the air and magically summon a boat to travel on."

"Then where do you think they are?" Wolf Hawk asked, again searching his old grandfather's eyes.

"I cannot say, but I can tell you this. You will eventually have them to do with as you please," Talking Bird said flatly. "Go. Search again. Be patient. Even if it takes you many sunrises and sunsets, in time you will find these men and your vengeance will finally be achieved."

"But what do you suggest that I do?" Wolf Hawk asked.

"The search for the wrongdoers might take much longer than you wish it to take, but in time, it will be the killers who will step into a trap," Talking Bird said, slowly smiling. His eyes twinkled as he gazed into Wolf Hawk's. "This trap I speak of will not be the sort that killed the young braves, but one that will assure your vengeance."

Again he reached out from beneath his blanket and patted Wolf Hawk on the knee. "Be patient," he softly advised. "Be patient, for it will happen, my grandson."

They embraced, then Wolf Hawk returned home. As he reached his own lodge, he realized there was one more chore left to be done. The deadly traps were piled up outside the entrance-way of his tepee. He had promised his warriors that he, himself, would dispose of them.

He put all of the traps into a canoe, then boarded it himself. He lifted his paddle and guided the canoe out to the center of the river, where the water ran deepest. One by one he threw the traps overboard, until there were none left.

The water was now quiet as the moon painted its glow on the surface, spreading its light over the ripples in the wake of Wolf Hawk's canoe as he headed back toward shore.

He smiled at the knowledge that those traps would never be used again by the hunters.

"Now to make you pay for your crime," he whispered.

Chapter Nine

Many a man is making friends with death,
Even as I speak—
                    —Edna St. Vincent Millay

"You dumb cluck, I'm freezin' to death," Jeb growled out to Clint as they waded out of the water, onto land. "Some idea you had to hide in those rushes by the edge of the river."

"You're still alive, ain't cha?" Clint said, trembling from the cold, himself. "If we hadn't jumped into the water and hid in those thick, tall rushes when we heard the Injun comin' on his horse, we'd probably be dead. Our scalps would even now be hanging on poles in that savage's lodge."

"I just wish we could've gotten farther upriver before almost bein' caught by the savage," Jeb said, running his fingers through his dripping red hair and pushing it back from his face. "But I never thought about bein' tracked. I thought we'd be safe stayin' hidden in the forest beside the river while we waited for someone to come by in a boat. But there hasn't been a single boat since we got here. I think we're stuck, Clint. We might as well let the Injun have us now instead of later. What's the difference?"

"The difference is that while we're still alive

and breathing and in possession of our scalps, we have a chance of gettin' out of this mess," Clint said, the moon's light showing a glower on his whiskered face. "Jeb, let's hightail it outta here. Let's get as far upriver as we can. I don't 'spect the Injun to search this area again. There ain't no reason to. He didn't find us, so he must believe we're gone."

"If we make fresh tracks now, he'll be able to find us and I think he will come lookin' again," Jeb said as he grabbed his rifle from its hiding place amid thick forsythia bushes while Clint grabbed his own.

They started walking quickly alongside the river, staying in the shadows of the trees.

"Did you see that huge bird awhile back?" Clint said, huffing and puffing as Jeb started walking faster. "I ain't never seen anything like it. What sort of bird could live to get that big? The wing span reached so far, I couldn't even say how wide it was."

He shuddered. "And its eyes," he said. "I saw the glitter in those eyes as they picked up the moon's glow in 'em."

"Yes, I saw that, too," Jeb panted, sprinting now. His clothes were drying on him as he moved. "I felt as though if that bird had seen us, it might've dropped from the sky and sunk its claws in us and carried us away. You know, I've heard Injun myths where people turn into birds. Ain't you?"

"Hogwash," Clint growled out. "If you said that to anyone else but me, they'd say you was born daft. So just shut up such talk as that. It was only the shadows that made the bird seem so huge. Nothing more. Now concentrate on escapin' the wrath of those Injuns. Keep an eye out for a boat."

Suddenly Jeb stopped.

He reached out and grabbed Clint by the arm.

He sniffed long and hard.

Then he looked at Clint. "I smell smoke," he said, his voice filled with a sudden bone-chilling fear. "Where there's smoke, there's people. Lordie, Clint, what if we've gone in the direction of the In-jun village? We might be walkin' straight into a trap."

"Funny use of words," Clint said, glancing over at Jeb. "Don't poke fun, Jeb. This ain't no time to compare anything with traps. We've left a few behind us in the forest. You know that we also left behind some mighty good pelts."

"I ain't jestin'," Jeb said, his eyes peering through the darkness, seeing dark shadows and threatening shapes everywhere the moon did not reach. "I don't know what to do, which way to go, for we truly don't know what lies ahead of us. Smellin' smoke ain't good, Clint. It ain't good at all."

"Well, we sure ain't gonna know who set that fire if we don't go farther and investigate," Clint mumbled. "Hurry into the darkness of the trees. Move onward with caution. Only thing I know is that I'm all turned 'round. I can't tell where on earth we are, or who we might run across any minute now. I just know that smoke can mean two different things to us. It can mean we're too close to Injuns, or we've come upon some traveler makin' camp for the night."

"I'm afraid to see who it is," Jeb said, fear in his squinting eyes. "I'm afraid we might be takin' our last breaths of life. If it's the Injuns, we're doomed. Doomed. What if it is Injuns?"

"We won't know until we go and see, now will we?" Clint said, clasping his right hand harder around his rifle. "Come on. Don't become a baby on me now. We need each other to get out of this pickle."

"Yeah, each other," Jeb mumbled. "If you want to know the truth, I wish I'd never laid eyes on you. You've been nothin' but trouble for me. Yeah, I like the pelts we have stored at the old fort, such an ungodly amount for only one day, and I have you to thank for helpin' me with the hunt, but I doubt now that we'll ever be able to take 'em out of here. More'n likely, the Injuns'll find 'em as they hunt for us."

"Just shut up your whinin'," Clint spat back at Jeb. "Come on. Time's wastin'. If those who built the fire are friends, then we finally have a way out of this mess. We can come back later for the pelts. No one knows where they're hid. Even the Injuns wouldn't know where to find them. They are hid down in the darkness of that underground room, and the trapdoor that leads down there is well hid beneath a rug and a heavy piece of furniture."

"Clint, look yonder," Jeb said, reaching out and grabbing one of Clint's arms. "Am I seein' things or is that a scow moored at the banks of the river? Look at that thing. It seems to have everything on it, even what looks like a small house of sorts. I wonder who it belongs to?"

"Come on, let's hurry to it," Clint said, yanking his arm away from Jeb's hand. "This is what we've been prayin' for . . . a way to escape this god awful forest where Injuns are out for our blood."

"It's so big," Jeb whined. "I don't think we can man it."

He squinted as he stepped from the shadows, to survey the scow. His eyes widened in surprise when he saw exactly where their flight had taken them.

The old fort where they'd left their pelts!

There it was as plain as day beneath the bright light of the full moon.

And by the light of the moon he also saw smoke spiraling skyward from somewhere inside the fort.

"The pelts," he gasped. "Clint, there's the fort. Those who arrived in that scow have taken refuge in the fort. What if they . . . ?"

"What's most important is our own hides. To hell with the pelts," Clint said tightly. "And chances are those people have no idea they are sittin' on top of a gold mine. Just remember how well we hid 'em. Mere travelers won't even think about treasures lyin' beneath their feet. They have stopped here for one thing. To rest until they travel onward tomorrow. But there's one thing they don't know."

He chuckled beneath his breath. "They won't

have anything to travel onward on," he said. "We're takin' that scow, Jeb. Now. Come with me. I don't see no one standin' watch. Let's get away while the gettin' is good. We'll travel on to good ol' Saint Louie, wait until we feel it's safe to return, then come back and grab those hides."

Jeb saw the logic in what Clint said and ran with him to the scow.

Both placed their rifles on board, then worked at untying the two ropes that held the scow in place.

When the ropes were finally loosened, they flipped them onto the deck, then shoved and pushed, panting from the exertion it took, until the scow was floating free. Then they jumped on board and guided it to the center of the river with the two huge oars.

As they moved downriver in the direction of St. Louis, they kept a close eye on the land, still fearful of Indians.

The farther they traveled, the safer and more self-assured they became.

Suddenly Clint bent over in a rush of laughter. "We did it," he said between his snorts of laughter. "We fooled those damn savages. Now they'll never be able to avenge the deaths of those two young braves."

"Vengeance is mine, sayeth the Lord," Jeb shouted, mockingly quoting a passage from the Bible. "Well, savages, seems the good Lord above knows more about vengeance than you ever will."

Something made Clint look quickly heavenward.

He would never forget that wide span of wings on the bird he and Jeb had seen. If that bird showed up now and dove down toward them on this scow, he'd sure enough wet his breeches.

He made himself think about other things and looked straight ahead. As the scow made its way through the water, Clint's arms began to ache at the work it took to keep the craft moving steadily along.

He'd never done much physical labor before. Trappin' was his life.

Well, at least for now, he'd have to work, and work hard. His life might depend on rowing this scow to St. Louis.

Back at the fort, Mia stirred in her sleep. She awakened with a start, then gazed over at her father.

The moon was streaming through a window onto her father's face.

When she saw how peacefully he was sleeping and noticed that his breathing was no longer so labored, she sighed with relief. She drew her blanket more snugly around her shoulders and drifted off to sleep again.

Not far from her, the birdcage sat with its door gaping open, its cover not in its usual place.

Tiny was awake and had seen Mia checking on her pa. She hadn't even thought to check on her canary.

Oh, but didn't she have a surprise waitin' for her on the morrow!

Oh, what a relief it would be not to have that bird squawkin' and singin' anymore on the scow as they traveled onward to St. Louis.

Ah, but wouldn't it be peaceful!

He looked toward the closed door of the cabin. Something had awakened him a few minutes ago.

It was a sound that seemed to be coming from the direction of the river. It had sounded like hushed voices of men.

But surely he was imagining things. No one was near.

He shrugged, wiped at his dry mouth with a hand, then settled back in his blankets.

He fell into a deep, restful sleep, unaware that in the morning his entire world would be turned upside down.

Chapter Ten

Then farewell care, and farewell woe,—
I will no longer pine.

—Sir John Suckling

The early morning sunshine crept into the window, dappling its soft light onto Mia's face and awakening her.

Yawning and stretching her arms above her head, she was momentarily disoriented as to where she was. It came to her suddenly when she looked over and saw her father, whose face seemed paler than the last time she had looked at him.

It frightened her to hear that his breathing was now more shallow than she had ever heard it before. The thought of losing him caused a painful ache in the pit of her stomach.

As she watched him sleep, she was catapulted back to the day her mother had told Mia that they were heading back to St. Louis, and how this would be the last time they would take one of their yearly treks on the river. Because of Mia's father's failing health, their family was going to return to their home and never board a scow again.

It had been a glorious day beside the river that

morning, as they sat near the fire before setting out on the scow toward home.

Mia had looked forward to staying in one place year-round. She would never forget how broadly she had smiled as her mother told her that they would sell their scow on the St. Louis riverbank.

That would make everything final. Mia couldn't have been happier with the decision.

But her family would keep one mode of river travel in case it was needed . . . the longboat that trailed along behind the scow each day, which had her name painted on it. Her father just couldn't part with everything that had to do with his river travels, especially not the boat that he had named after his daughter.

When they had boarded the scow that day, Mia had felt as though she were floating on clouds instead of water as they headed toward St. Louis. Even her canary had seemed to understand that one day soon it would be home.

"My sweet Georgina," Mia whispered to herself.

She looked quickly over at the cage.

At that moment she realized that something was not right. Usually at this time of the morning, Georgina could be heard fussing softly behind her cover, for the canary was always anxious for the cloth to be removed so that she could see Mia and the fresh seed and water her mistress gave her each morning.

Something grabbed Mia's heart, like a hand

squeezing it, when she saw the cover on the cage was not at all the way she had left it.

And then she noticed that the door was ajar. Mia never left the door ajar!

She could not get to the cage quickly enough. She brushed aside the blanket and leapt up. When she peered inside the cage, remorse swept through her. Georgina was most definitely not there.

Tears sprang to her eyes over her loss. Then it came to her like a lightning bolt from the heavens that there was no way Georgina could have opened that door, for Mia always double-checked it before going to bed each night.

Only after seeing that it was secure would she go to bed, for if anything happened to her bird, a part of her would die.

Yes, the bird had become especially precious to her since her mother's death. Georgina had helped lift Mia from the horrible sorrow that came after burying her mother along the banks of the Rush River.

Having to leave her mother there, oh, so alone, was something that Mia still could hardly bear to think about.

And now?

Had she also lost her bird?

And her father—how long would she have him as a part of her life?

His health seemed to be worsening by the minute!

Yes, her world seemed to be tumbling all around her. She felt as if she were on a small island by herself, with no happiness left inside her.

When she examined the cage, she was certain there was no way that Georgina could have escaped without assistance. Someone had lifted the cover and opened the door for the bird, and it surely had not been done inside the cabin, or Georgina would have found her way to Mia and settled down beside her. The bird loved Mia so much that she was sure Georgina wouldn't have chosen to fly away.

Mia looked quickly at the door of the cabin. It was closed!

That meant someone had opened the door, carried the cage outside, and then sent Georgina to a freedom that might mean her death.

Georgina had been tiny when Mia's mother had given her the bird. All the canary knew was the cage, the food and water she found there, and Mia, who gave her these things. Mia meant safety and food and love.

As long as Mia was there to care for her, Georgina's world was secure. But now? Oh, Lord, where was Georgina, and who . . . ?

She looked quickly at Tiny and found him awake and gazing at her with a strange look of triumph.

"You . . . !" Mia cried, awakening her father with her outburst of anger. "Tiny! You did this. You carried the cage outside and opened the door. How did you get Georgina from it? I know she wouldn't fly through that door, for the cage was a safe haven to her!"

She stomped over to where Tiny was sitting up on his blanket, his eyes squinting into Mia's with a mischievous glint.

"How could you do this?" she cried, then slapped him hard on the face.

Tiny yelped and reached a hand to his face. He glared at Mia. "You little . . ." he began, but didn't finish what he'd started to say. He knew better, for her father was now sitting up on his blanket, giving Tiny a cold stare.

"To hell with you both," Tiny blurted out. He threw the blanket that he had slept under aside, and still fully clothed, rushed from the cabin.

Mia stared blankly at the open door, then the cage, and then at her father.

"I told you, Papa, that he was a horrible man, and now look at what he has done," she sobbed. "My sweet Georgina. Surely she did not survive the night in the forest."

"Darlin', I'll buy you another bird when we get back home," Harry said. He groaned with the effort it took to get to his feet.

"There could never be a bird like Georgina," Mia said, hurrying to his assistance when she saw that his knees almost buckled beneath him. "Papa, please lie back down. Rest while I fix us something to eat. You need to eat to keep your strength."

Suddenly the air was split with the sound of Tiny's yells.

"Did he say that the scow is missing?" her father asked, gripping Mia's arm as he turned and gazed toward the open door. "Mia, did . . . I . . . hear right?"

"Oh, Papa, you did," Mia cried. "You did. Please lie down and I'll go and see about it."

"Help me outside," Harry said, his voice drawn. "Mia, help . . . me . . . outside."

"Papa, please . . ." she softly pleaded.

"Mia, do as you are told," Harry snapped in a tone that Mia was not used to hearing from her father.

She was afraid that this latest turn of events might cause him to have another heart attack!

"Papa, please settle down," Mia softly encouraged when she turned toward him and saw his face.

Earlier it had been ashen. Now she saw flushed cheeks and purplish, quivering lips.

"I've got to see for myself," Harry said, a sudden sob catching in his throat. "That scow. It's our only way home, Mia. And it's been . . . everything to me. I'll never forget our adventures on it. Your mother, ah, what memories we shared on that scow."

"I know, Papa, but please don't get any more upset than you already are when you see that the scow is gone," Mia said, gently taking her father by the elbow and ushering him slowly to the door.

When they both stepped outside and went to the gate of the fort, there was no sign of the scow. They both gasped with horror at the same time.

"Someone came and took it," Harry said dispiritedly.

He leaned on Mia, his full weight almost pulling her down to the ground. "Oh, Lord, Mia, what are we to do?" he asked, his voice full of despair.

Tiny came to them.

For the first time since Mia had known him, he seemed sympathetic . . . and afraid.

"What are we to do now?" he asked, gazing intently into Harry's eyes. "We're stranded. We're damn stranded."

"Tiny, go and stand beside the river. Flag down the first boat you see working its way up or down the river," Harry said, his voice even weaker than moments earlier.

He leaned even harder on Mia. "That's all we can do," he said, his face flushed. "We have no other recourse except to hope someone comin' on that river will have mercy on us."

"But . . ." Tiny began. He stopped when Harry glared at him.

"Go and watch for someone to come by," Harry ordered flatly. "When you see anyone, Tiny, anyone, flag 'em down. Or else we are here to stay. With the few provisions we have, we won't last long, and I'm not able to walk farther than this gate."

"I guess you know that we are at the mercy of any Indian who might happen along, too," Tiny said, nervously picking at his whiskers.

"That's another reason we should be certain to

find someone who will have mercy on us as soon as we can, someone who will offer us a ride on their boat," Mia said, already turning her father to walk back to the cabin.

She looked over her shoulder at Tiny. "Tiny, please keep a close watch for a boat . . . and any signs of Indians," she said. "For now we've no choice but to stay put and hope for the best."

"I'm hungry," Tiny growled.

"I'll fix us some breakfast, some oats from what's left of the supply we took off the boat, but you'll have to eat it without sugar, for I left that canister on the scow, not thinking someone would steal our boat and everything on it," Mia said.

She went on through the gate with her father as Tiny meandered down to the riverbank.

Cursing, Tiny kicked at the rocks along the shore, then nervously looked over his shoulder into the dark shadows of the forest.

He knew that they were sitting ducks if any Indians should come along.

He gazed up at the smoke spiraling from inside the fort's walls, knowing that Mia had put more wood on the fire so that she could prepare the oats.

If an Indian got wind of that smoke . . .

Suddenly he felt too afraid to stay out there by himself. He sneaked back inside the walls of the fort, but made certain not to let Mia or her father see him. If he heard any noise down by the river, such as a boat might make as it passed, he would hurry out there and flag it down.

Otherwise, he would protect his own hide. He wouldn't be a sitting duck like Mia's mother had been on the scow, downed by an Indian's deadly arrow!

Chapter Eleven

Heart, are you great enough
For a love that never tires?
O, heart, are you great
Enough for love?

—Alfred, Lord Tennyson

Wolf Hawk had left his tepee before dawn and had gone from lodge to lodge to awaken his warriors.

He had slept hardly at all through the night and had decided during those waking hours that he could not truly rest until he found the ones who had caused the deaths of the Bird Clan's innocent young braves.

Although his earlier search had led him to a standstill at the river, he would not give up so quickly.

Traveling on horseback, Wolf Hawk and his warriors set out again through the forest. They would take the entire day to search for the trappers, and if they were not found today, perhaps tomorrow!

One day he would have his vengeance.

Somehow, some day, he would come face-to-face with the two white men and he would make them pay for their crimes against the fallen youths.

It was now just past daybreak.

The early, soft rays of the sun streamed through the foliage of the trees overhead as Wolf Hawk traveled onward.

Robins warbled and sang their songs throughout the forest, making everything seem serene and peaceful, but Wolf Hawk was far from serene.

His insides were tight.

His need for vengeance was like a hot poker in the pit of his belly, burning, sending him onward through the huge oaks, elms, and the tall spruces that gave off such a wonderful scent.

Here and there squirrels scampered from limb to limb, startled by the noise of the horses' hooves.

Some ignored the commotion, remaining beneath the trees, frantically digging through the dirt and rotting leaves to uncover a nut they had planted there earlier, which they could consume for their breakfast today.

When Wolf Hawk saw two dark eyes peering through the brush, he recognized them as those of a deer. He saw that he was right when it suddenly leapt out into the open and fled into the darker recesses of the forest.

Wolf Hawk's warriors paid no attention to it. They carried their quivers of arrows on their backs, and long bows over their shoulders. All wore knives sheathed at their waists, and all were attired in breechclouts and moccasins, their long black hair fluttering in the wind as they continued to wind their way through the forest. Their eyes took in each and every movement, even the slightest stirring of leaves overhead, but they were not hunting for deer or any other animal.

Their jaws tight, their chins firm, they were intent on hunting the evil trappers.

None thought that the trappers could completely elude them. They did not believe that their Earthmaker above would allow such atrocities to go unpunished.

Suddenly Wolf Hawk caught the scent of smoke in the air. He raised a fist, his silent order for the warriors to stop.

Wolf Hawk's eyes scanned the forest ahead of them. Through a break in the trees just up ahead he saw the old abandoned fort. The smoke was spiraling heavenward from somewhere inside the walls of the fort.

Someone had most certainly taken shelter in the fort, and he hoped that it was the trappers. If so, the killers were doomed.

They would not slip past his warriors. Even now he was giving them quiet commands where to go and place themselves. His plan was to surround the fort, to stop anyone who might try to leave.

When all of his men were in place, and he himself stood at the entrance, where the gate stood wide open, Wolf Hawk shouted a warning to those who were inside.

"You are surrounded!" Wolf Hawk shouted, his hand clutching his rifle, ready to fire should it become necessary. "Show yourselves! Now!"

He watched and waited, then spotted movement at the door of the cabin.

His eyes widened when he saw that it was not a man, but a beautiful, slightly built, white woman.

And she stood alone in the door, making him wonder if those who were with her were too cowardly to come outside with her.

"Please don't hurt us," Mia cried, terrified that she might be experiencing the last moments of her life.

And she was so afraid for her father, whose body and heart were too weak for confrontations such as this!

As for Tiny, he was worthless, a coward. Mia's father came and stood at her side, but Tiny shrank as far back against the far wall as possible, staying hidden.

"What do you want of us?" Mia called out to the Indian who seemed in charge. She noted his air of command, his sculpted features and muscled body. "My father and I are innocent of any wrongdoing against you. We are stranded. During the night someone stole our boat . . . our river scow."

She glanced over at her father, who had crept to her side. She saw his paleness and frailty as he stood there now, afraid, his arm quivering as he held it around her waist.

Mia directed her words again to the Indian who seemed to be in charge. He stood apart and in front of the others, his dark eyes gazing intently at her.

"My father is ill," Mia said, swallowing hard. "Please do nothing that will cause him to have another attack."

Wolf Hawk was pleased by the woman's strong will. She spoke courageously to him, whereas most women would cower and shy away from a strange man. He could not help noticing how beautiful and petite she was. Wolf Hawk did not want to make her feel threatened by him and his warriors.

All he wanted was those who had taken two of his young braves' lives.

He stepped forward, but stopped when he saw her father's eyes grow wide with fear. The old man seemed ready to pass out, and his knees looked as though they were ready to buckle beneath him.

"I am Chief Wolf Hawk of the Bird Clan of the Winnebago tribe," he stated. "I come in peace. I only ask for answers from you. If what you say proves your innocence, you will be left alone by us. Tell me first what your name is, and how many are with you besides your father."

"My name is Mia . . . Mia Collins, and this is my father, whose name is Harry," she murmured.

She was trying so hard to be courageous, for she had always heard that Indians rewarded courage and bravery.

"You have not spoken of anyone else—does that mean that you and your father are alone?" Wolf Hawk asked, losing some of his stiffness as he spoke.

He was beginning to believe that there were no trappers there.

This young woman did not seem to be someone who spoke lies easily.

"There is only one more person in our party,"

Mia said, her spine stiffening at the thought of Tiny Brown cowering inside the cabin, afraid to show his face. "His name is Tiny Brown. He is my father's assistant, who helped man our scow . . . a scow we no longer have. As I have already told you, it . . . it . . . was stolen in the night. We have been left stranded here."

Something about the white woman, her innocence, her ability to speak with him, an Indian, so easily—even though most white women were terrified of men with red skin—made Wolf Hawk believe that she was not lying.

But he did not want her to know that he trusted her. Perhaps she was able to lie while looking someone square in the eye. He would practice restraint; he would not allow her, yet, to know that he trusted her.

Trust had to be gained.

A search of the cabins would prove whether or not she deserved to be trusted.

"You say that your party numbers only three?" Wolf Hawk said stiffly. "My warriors will search all of the buildings and see if you lie, or tell truths."

He looked over his shoulder at his warriors. "I will stay with the woman and her father while you search," he said stiffly. "Go to each cabin. Make a thorough search. Soon we shall know if this woman tells the truth, or is skilled at lying."

"I have told you, there are only the three of us," Mia said, worrying about her father. He was standing perfectly still, and was strangely quiet.

She could feel his weakness as he clung to her. And she could hear his shallow breathing. It sounded the way he breathed when he was about to have one of his attacks!

"Please believe me," Mia begged. "My father . . ."

Wolf Hawk saw how desperate she seemed to be, and wondered whether she was truly worried about her father, or afraid his warriors would find others hiding in the fort.

"Search carefully," he shouted at the warriors who were already going in and out of the other cabins.

The woman truly did seem concerned about her father, and Wolf Hawk thought that surely she wasn't pretending.

"The search will be quick," he hurriedly advised. "If you tell truths, then we will leave you to yourselves."

Mia didn't know how she felt about being left alone without a way to leave this place, yet she realized that it was foolish to consider this Indian someone who would concern himself about white people and their troubles.

It was surely crazy to think of asking this Indian for help. She knew that most Indians despised the ground that white people walked on.

"May I take my father inside so that he can return to his pallet on the floor?" Mia asked softly, pleading with her green eyes for understanding.

Wolf Hawk was just about to tell her that she could return her father to a more comfortable place, but was stopped when one of his warriors came running toward him, an armload of pelts held before him.

"These pelts were surely hidden here by the trappers!" Blue Sky exclaimed as he stopped directly in front of Wolf Hawk.

Wolf Hawk's eyes went wide with surprise as he reached out and ran a hand over the plush softness of the pelts.

"There are many," Blue Sky said, looking over his shoulder as other warriors came carrying more and more pelts. "We found them hidden beneath a trap door in yonder cabin."

Seeing that the woman had not been truthful, and surprised that she was such a skillful liar, Wolf Hawk stepped around the warriors and stopped directly in front of Mia.

"You lie," he growled out. He nodded at another warrior. "Go inside. Find those who are surely hiding in there. Bring them out to me. Surely there are two, not one, as the woman indicated."

"There is only one man in there and he has nothing to do with trapping," Mia cried as two warriors brushed past her and her father and went inside the cabin. "He . . . helped . . . my father on our scow."

"You lie so easily," Wolf Hawk said stiffly. "Did you know that not only animals have died in your dreadful traps, but also two young braves who got trapped in those jaws of death!"

"Died . . . oh, no, please don't think I . . . we . . . had anything to do with such as that," Mia cried.

"We knew nothing of these pelts. When we arrived, to rest for the night away from the river, we chose this cabin without looking at any others. We knew not of any pelts being hidden there. We know nothing about trappers. When we arrived here, we looked only in this cabin. All we wanted was a place to rest. My father . . . he . . . isn't a well man."

Wolf Hawk glanced over at the woman's father again, seeing that he seemed to be getting worse by the minute. His shoulders were slumped and his breathing had become painfully shallow.

He wanted to believe this woman and offer to help her father, but how could he now trust anything she said?

How could he have any feelings for this elderly man when two of his own people, young braves who had had a lifetime ahead of them, were dead, and surely because of these white people!

Suddenly the warriors who had been sent inside the cabin came out, forcing Tiny ahead of them with hard shoves.

"There was only this one man in the cabin. We have found no others in the fort," Blue Sky reported.

"And he is who I said he was," Mia tried to explain. "He is only with me and my father because he helped row our scow."

Tiny said nothing, only cowered in the Indian's grip, his eyes pleading silently with her to make the Indians understand who he was . . . most definitely not a trapper!

"You still lie to me after we found proof of your dishonesty?" Wolf Hawk growled out. "Tell the whole truth now, white woman. If this tiny man is who you say he is, then where are the others? I know that there were two more because I found two horses abandoned in the forest. Surely the men came back here and are hiding even now as we speak. Are there other trapdoors where they might be hiding?"

"Oh, what can I say now to make you believe me?" Mia said, tears filling her eyes. "We were traveling on our scow down the Rush River on our way back home, to St. Louis. We stopped for the night. While we were sleeping, someone stole our scow. Surely it was those men you are speaking about."

"That could not be so," Wolf Hawk objected. "Trappers would not leave behind a prime catch like these pelts that we found." He took one step closer to Mia and her father. "It is time to stop this game you are playing . . ."

At that moment Mia's father gasped, grabbed at his chest, then fell to her feet.

"Papa!" she cried as she dropped to her knees beside him.

She checked his pulse and could feel none. He was dead!

He had suffered a massive heart attack this time. And there was only one person to blame: that vicious, heartless Indian chief who wouldn't listen to reason!

She glared up at him through her tears. "You

caused this," she cried. "You frightened my father to death! Do you hear me? He is dead! His heart has failed him!"

Wolf Hawk was stunned by what had just happened.

The white man had died right before his eyes, and it did seem that fright had killed him.

Yet Wolf Hawk refused to feel guilt over the death of someone who was a part of the scheme that had led to two of his young braves' deaths.

If this woman had told him the truth from the beginning, perhaps her father would still be alive.

"Please leave," Mia said, sobbing. "Don't you see that you have done enough here? I have lost my father. What more could you want from me? I have nothing, nothing now. My mother is already dead, shot down by an Indian's deadly arrow. And now my father? Oh, please leave. Please, please leave. The men you are searching for are surely long gone . . . on my family's scow. I have told you more than once that it was stolen during the night. When you find the scow, you will surely find your trappers."

"And you think I should believe that?" Wolf Hawk said stiffly. He nodded toward her father. "I will give you time with your father, but then you and the tiny man must come with me and my warriors to my village. That will draw the other two men there to rescue you. It will be their second mistake, for I will not allow myself to be fooled by a mere woman."

He looked her slowly up and down, then gazed

into her eyes. "What man could leave not only the pelts behind, but also you?" he said thickly. "You are beautiful, and though you are so small, you have the spirit of a wolf.

"We will take not only you to the village, but also the pelts. That will be enough to eventually lure them there. When they do come, they will get far more than they expect."

Mia saw the uselessness in begging him any more. She closed her eyes for a moment, trying to block out the terrible picture of her father lying there, dead, then looked at him again.

"Papa, oh, Papa, what am I to do?" she whispered.

Chapter Twelve

Sometimes too hot the eye of heaven shines,
And often is his gold complexion dimm'd;
And every fair from fair sometime declines,
By chance or nature's changing course
untrimm'd.

—William Shakespeare

Mia was so distraught over her father's death, she found it hard to go on. She was thankful that at least the young chief was allowing her to bury her father before she was taken to his village as a captive.

Mia had no idea what lay ahead of her. She knew nothing of any Indian tribe's habits, except for what she had read of terrible atrocities they had committed against white people out West.

She had also read accounts of the cavalry slaughtering huge numbers of Indians at a time, men, women, and children, alike. Part of her did not blame them for fighting back in any way that they could.

As she knelt beside her father for a moment longer, she cast a smoldering glance over her shoulder at Wolf Hawk. He was standing several feet away from her, watching her along with his warriors.

"Please?" she suddenly blurted out. "Can't you go and stand somewhere else as I say a prayer over my father? Can you not be decent enough to let me be, as I . . . I . . . bury my father? You are responsible for his death by frightening him into a heart attack. At least give him the respect that is due him, for he did not have a mean bone in his body. He never would have done anything to harm you or your people. He was a gentle, loving man."

She wiped tears from her eyes as she gazed directly into the young chief's eyes. "You have lost someone dear to you," she said, her voice softer. "The two young braves. Did you not have a time of mourning for them? Please allow me the privacy to mourn the one I love . . . and have lost."

Wolf Hawk listened with his heart. There was so much about this fragile woman that made him believe that she spoke the truth when she said she had had nothing to do with the traps that had killed the two braves.

Yet the evidence of the pelts was against her. He could not give up the chance that the trappers would come to claim her once she was taken captive to his village.

No, he would not allow the sweetness of her voice, nor the pleading look in her lovely green eyes, to sway him from what he must do. Nonetheless, he did understand that she needed moments alone with her father. It was the only decent thing to do; to give her those moments.

He said nothing, but nodded to his warriors

and stepped away her. He led them to the entrance of the fort, where the gate stood open, and waited there. From this position, he could still see her kneeling over the body of her father just outside the cabin.

He could also keep an eye on the tiny man who stood somewhat away from the woman and her father. He saw no respect whatsoever in the man's eyes, nor sadness. All that Wolf Hawk could identify was annoyance when the tiny, whiskered man gazed down at the woman whose name was Mia.

Wolf Hawk's instincts told him that this tiny person was not a man of good heart. He was the one that Wolf Hawk would question at length once they returned to their village.

He would leave Mia alone to mourn her father while he took this man, called rightfully enough by the name Tiny, and question him until he finally told the truth.

"Thank you," Mia murmured to Wolf Hawk. "I . . . won't . . . be long."

Wolf Hawk nodded, then turned to his warriors. "Blue Sky, go and direct the others to return to the entrance of the fort. We must prepare several travois to transport the pelts we found here back to our village. Tell them to hurry, for we shall all be leaving soon for our village."

Blue Sky nodded and hurried to do his chief's bidding.

Wolf Hawk turned again and watched the woman as she stood up and went to the small man. He bent his ear in their direction, to hear what they were saying, for he did not want anything to get past him. He had given this woman his permission to bury her father. Nothing more.

He saw the tiny man go into the cabin and return with a rusty shovel in his hands. He could hear the woman pleading with the little man to please dig the grave for her.

"Mia, I'll dig this damn grave for you, but hear me well when I tell you that I am sneaking away from this place at my first opportunity," Tiny said just loudly enough for Mia to hear.

She watched as he began to dig the dirt out of the ground, seemingly only an inch at a time. Again she was reminded of what a useless man he was and regretted the moment her father had hired him. She had wondered sometimes if he was running from the law, for he seemed the shiftless sort who might have done something that warranted jail time.

"Did you hear me, Mia?" Tiny demanded, pausing to rest for a moment on the shovel. "I'm sneaking away when I see the chance. You can stay and face the music, yourself. I'm not paying for the wrongful acts of others and I don't give a damn what happens to you. I was paid to steer the scow to St. Louis, nothin' more. It's not my fault that all your plans have gone awry."

Mia stiffened as he talked. Tiny was now leaning lazily against the shovel instead of digging.

She was afraid the young chief might come at any moment and order them away before the grave was dug and her father laid to rest in it.

"You lazy coward," she hissed out. "I don't care what you do after you get that grave dug. You are a useless, horrible human being."

"Oh?" Tiny said, lifting his eyebrows. He threw the shovel at her. "If you're going to call me useless, why should I waste my time digging a grave? You do it yourself. Your father was nothing to me. Do you hear? Nothing."

Mia gasped at his words. She knew the ground was hard and doubted that she could finish digging a grave large enough for her father.

But seeing that Tiny meant what he was saying, and that he had gone back inside the cabin, leaving her alone to complete the chore, she began crying. She tried to dig the grave, but found it impossible.

She knew that she must, though, so she continued to chop at the earth, only dislodging tiny bits of dirt.

Wolf Hawk saw what had happened.

He watched the young woman trying so hard to dig through the hardened ground, but saw how little she succeeded. He knew that she must bury her father in order to mourn him properly. Wolf Hawk was a man of religion and understood how one must care for the dead. He could not allow her to suffer any longer.

He left his warriors and hurried inside the cabin to confront Tiny. "You are not a man, but instead a woman," he said, his jaw tight. "A man would not make a woman do his work. Get out there. Dig. Prove that you are a man."

Tiny could not help being afraid of the young chief, but there was nothing on this earth that would make him do the work he had said Mia must do.

It was true that her father was nothing to him. Why must he behave as though he cared by helping dig the grave? Tiny squared his shoulders and glared right back into Wolf Hawk's midnight-dark eyes.

"You do not do as you are told?" Wolf Hawk said, leaning his face down into Tiny's. "Must I force you? Do you wish to be humiliated more than you are already are? Shall I march you bodily out there to dig that grave?"

Tiny's will bent a little under the wrath of the chief's words, but he just would not let this red man coerce him.

And he needed time alone. He needed this time to make his escape through a back window. He was absolutely not going to be taken to the Indian village and possibly tortured for answers he did not have about those trappers.

He preferred to be stubborn now in the hope of finding a way to escape. He had heard the chief order his warriors to the front of the fort. This might be the opportunity he needed.

"I heard the woman call you a coward," Wolf Hawk spat out. "You are worse than that. You are a nobody."

Wolf Hawk walked away while Tiny glared at his back. As soon as he was alone, Tiny hurried to the back of the cabin, crawled through the window, then made a mad dash toward the fort's rear walls. He was relieved to see that there was enough space between some of the boards to escape through.

He would find some place to hide until the Indians departed; then he would watch the river for someone to rescue him.

Breathing hard, he ran and ran, all the while glancing time and again over his shoulder, relieved when no one gave chase. He made his way into the thickest part of the trees, searching for a place to hide.

While Tiny was making his escape, Wolf Hawk was speaking to Mia.

"Come with me where the earth is softer," Wolf Hawk said, gently taking the shovel from her.

Mia was stunned by his kindness, yet as she walked with him from the fort, she could not help feeling uncomfortable at his nearness.

He was a savage.

Her mother had been killed by a savage's arrow.

Who was to say that this very Indian had not shot the arrow? Or perhaps one of his warriors had taken it upon himself to kill a white person as vengeance for the lives of the many red people whose lives had been taken by soldiers.

The more she thought of this possibility, the more she did not want this Indian to dig her father's grave. It seemed sacrilegious, somehow.

Although she knew it would be almost impossible for her to dig a grave out of the hard, bone-dry ground, she just could not let this man do it. She told herself he was nothing but a savage, even though she had been taken by his handsomeness and his recent kindness.

"You don't need to dig my father's grave," Mia said, stepping up to Wolf Hawk. She reached a hand out toward him. "Give me the shovel. I need no man's help, especially not the very Indian who is responsible for my father's deadly heart attack."

Wolf Hawk was stung by her words, yet struck by her courage. It could not be easy for her to come up to him and face him with such bitter words. She knew that he was a powerful chief in command of many warriors, yet she, tiny thing that she was, did not hesitate to stand up to him.

He understood that it was necessary for her to dig the grave herself, to honor her father. He was a man who admired courage in a woman, and especially a woman who had such respect and love for her father.

He handed the shovel to Mia. "I urge you to make the grave here, beneath these trees," Wolf Hawk said. "It is a better place for your father's eternal rest."

Again stunned by his kindness, Mia stared at him for a moment. She realized that this was, indeed, the perfect place for her father's eternal rest. Wolf Hawk had led her to a shady grove of maples and elms.

Although the earth there was not as hard as inside the fort's walls, it was still difficult to dig into. But she would not break down and hand the shovel to Wolf Hawk. She was stubborn in that way . . . a trait her mother had deplored in Mia!

She did not look at him again as she struggled to dig the grave. Sweat dripped from her brow and wetted her dress. Her long auburn hair clung to her cheeks and brow.

She sighed heavily with relief when she felt the grave was deep enough to hold her father's body. Her arms and back ached from the hard work.

She laid the shovel aside and went back inside the fort to kneel beside her father.

She reached out a hand to his pale cheek, held her fingers there for a moment as she bent low and kissed his cold lips. Then slowly she reached for his arms to begin the dreaded task of dragging him to the grave.

Flashes of her mother being laid in the dirt some miles back came to her, causing a sob to rise from deep inside her, and tears to rush again from her eyes.

"Mama, Papa," she whispered. "How can this be? I no longer have either of you."

Before attempting to take her father's body to the grave, she looked heavenward. Although she felt Wolf Hawk's dark eyes on her, watching her every move, she murmured a soft prayer, then spoke a memorized verse from the Bible that she recalled her father speaking over her mother's grave.

Then, knowing that she had taken more time

than the Indian wanted to allow her, she stood up, bent low and grabbed her father's arms.

She grunted and groaned as she tried to pull his dead weight to the grave, but didn't succeed in budging him even one inch from the spot where he had fallen and died.

"No," she moaned in despair. She had never felt so helpless in her entire life, for she knew now that she could not do this alone, and she most certainly would not go inside the cabin and ask Tiny for any more help.

If she had to drag her father one inch at a time and stand in a pool of her own sweat from the effort, she would get her father buried. And she would do it by herself.

No matter what she must face as a young woman now alone in the world, she would, and with a lifted chin. She would not show an ounce of cowardice to these Indians, especially not this chief whom she blamed for causing her father's heart attack.

Wolf Hawk winced when he saw the trouble Mia was having transporting her father to his grave. But he could not help being proud of her for not asking anyone's assistance.

When Mia tried once more to move her father's body and could not even budge him, she dropped the shovel and sank to her knees. She put her face in her hands and cried.

She hated showing such weakness to these Indians, but she could not help it.

She felt totally helpless, for she knew that she could not complete this task alone.

Suddenly out of the corner of her eye she saw someone bend over on the opposite side of her father. She saw two powerful arms and hands reach beneath her father and pick him up from the ground as though his body weighed no more than a feather.

She slowly looked up and found herself staring into the eyes of Wolf Hawk as he met her gaze, then carried her father to the grave.

Oh, so much was exchanged between them in those brief moments. Mia was puzzled, for she felt strangely drawn to this man whose deeds did not match the harshness of his words. Instead, he was giving her a look that melted her heart because it was so full of caring and understanding.

It was at this moment that she realized this man would not harm her in any way; nor could he have been the one who had shot the arrow into her mother's body.

He had come and frightened her father, yes, but she knew that he had not intended for her father to die. He had come seeking those who had slain two innocent young braves.

Mia rose to her feet and went to kneel by the grave. Again she gazed with intense love at her father's lifeless body. Again she murmured a soft prayer.

When she stood and took up the shovel to begin shoveling the dirt over her father's body, each turn of the shovel was like a knife being thrust into her heart.

And when it was over and all that remained was a mound on the ground, she gave Wolf Hawk a questioning look.

"We must go now," Wolf Hawk said. "Are there some of your belongings that you would want to take with you? For you will not be allowed to return to this place, not once you are in my village."

The fact that she was most definitely going to be this man's captive gave Mia a chill and she questioned her earlier thoughts about him. Mia paused for a moment as their eyes met and held, then she shook her head as though coming out of a trance.

"Yes, I would like to take a few things with me," she murmured. "I won't be long."

"I will follow you," Wolf Hawk replied, not wanting to leave her alone with the tiny man who seemed so disrespectful to her.

Mia ignored Wolf Hawk, and hurried inside the cabin.

She paused, taking a last look at the empty birdcage. Oh, how she despised Tiny for releasing her canary to the wild . . . a bird that had no idea how to survive away from her cage, where she had been safe, loved, fed and watered.

She looked quickly away from the cage, for she didn't want to think of what might have happened to Georgina. She was another one of Mia's losses, adding to her heartbreak.

Mia started to gather up some things but suddenly realized that Tiny wasn't in the cabin!

Wolf Hawk had noticed his absence even before she did. He ran from the cabin and she could hear him shouting out orders to go and find the escaped prisoner.

She grimaced when she then heard the thundering of horse's hooves. The warriors were in pursuit of Tiny.

She closed her eyes so that she would not envision what might happen to him for attempting this escape. She believed he would pay dearly for trying to best these red men of the forest!

They knew the forest much better than he and would soon find him.

Wolf Hawk came back inside the cabin. "He will not have gotten far," he said. He helped Mia by picking up her travel bag and holding it open so she could drop what she wanted inside.

She smiled weakly at him as a way to thank him for helping her. So much had happened, she was beginning to feel numb.

She put what clothes she could in the bag, along with her hairbrush, her mama's Bible, and then something of her father's . . . a book of poetry that he had read oft times while relaxing on the first leg of the journey, before things began going wrong for them.

After her mother's burial, her father had never been the same. He had spent most of his time alone, smoking his pipe.

And now even his pipe was gone. It had fallen

into the river when her father had had one of his spells.

Oh, if only she at least had that piece of him, it would bring him close to her on those nights when she would miss him so much. The poetry book might help, but in truth, she knew she would never get used to not having him around.

"We should go now," Wolf Hawk said when he saw that she was no longer placing things in her bag. "We shall go to my village. Those who are searching for the tiny man will return once they have recaptured him."

Mia took one last look at the empty birdcage, then walked from the cabin.

She went to her father's grave. She needed one last moment with him. It just did not seem real to be leaving her father there all alone in the ground as she had been made to leave her mother.

Suddenly a terrible feeling of loneliness gripped her. She swayed and felt as though she might faint.

But a mighty, strong hand on her shoulder reminded her that she was not alone. Although this man was her enemy, she did not believe he would allow any true harm to come to her. The look in his eyes as she gazed into them showed too much gentleness.

She held her chin high and walked from the grave with him.

She then saw a travois attached to one of the warriors' horses. She was amazed at how many pelts were on it, piled high and secured with a rope.

She could only guess their value. She had been

at trading posts with her parents as they bought supplies while roaming the rivers. She had seen the coins and supplies that were exchanged for such pelts.

A shiver ran down her spine when she thought of the trappers and the loss they must be feeling at having to abandon this prime catch.

She had to believe they would not give it up so easily.

Surely they would return to retrieve the pelts. What would they do when they found them gone?

When they reached Wolf Hawk's horse, Mia stood back as he secured her travel bag on it. She sucked in a wild breath of fear when Wolf Hawk then lifted her onto the saddle and mounted behind her.

But soon her fear changed to something surprising. She could not help feeling a sensual thrill when Wolf Hawk reached his arm around her and held her in place against his hard body as he rode into the forest.

She fought these feelings, for she knew that she should hate this man. He was a savage and he was blaming her for something she had not done.

She couldn't believe that Tiny was so cowardly he had left her alone to fend for herself with these Indians.

As they continued on through the forest, Mia realized that she was entering a new phase in her life and wondered just where it might take her. She no longer felt like the same Mia.

She thought of her papa and mama together in the heavens. They were surely holding hands and smiling as they looked down at her, proud of her courage!

Chapter Thirteen

It well maybe that, in a difficult hour
Pinned down by pain and moaning for release,
Or nagged by want past resolution's power,
I mite be driven to sell you love for peace—
                    —Edna St. Vincent Millay

The journey to the village seemed endless to Mia as she rode on the horse with Wolf Hawk, but finally she saw many tepees through a break in the trees.

A sense of dread enveloped her, for she had never even seen an Indian village, much less entered one as a captive.

She would not allow herself to think the worst, but instead she sat straight and watched as the tepees grew closer and closer. When they entered the village, Indian women, men and children came to greet their chief and his warriors. But as they approached, they looked first at the white woman with their chief and then at the pelts on the travois and frowned with distaste.

And she understood why they had a sudden dislike for her. Surely they thought that she had something to do with the death of their two fallen braves, for she was the only white person who accompanied the pelts into the village. She was filled with a sudden apprehensiveness . . . a cold fear.

Wolf Hawk drew rein and those who were with him did the same. He gazed from one to the other of his people, recognizing apprehension and anger in their eyes and attitudes.

He understood.

He knew they believed this woman was involved in the deaths of their fallen youths. He had believed the same at first, and even now was unsure if she could ever be proven innocent.

If the trappers had fled this country from fear, with intentions of never returning, then he had a hard decision about this woman to make. Release her? Or keep her forever as his captive.

The latter possibility gave him much thought, for it was not the custom of his people to hold white captives.

Seeing how anxious his people were to understand why the woman had been brought to the village, Wolf Hawk nodded at them.

"My warriors, I will meet with those of you who stayed behind to protect our village," he said. "Then you can go to your families and give them the same explanation that I share with you. For now, I will say this . . . the pelts you see were found hidden at the old fort. We will use them to lure the trappers here. After they are captured, I shall hand the pelts over to you all to divide amongst yourselves. Keep what you want and trade what you wish to trade."

When all eyes remained directed on the

woman, he realized that explanation wasn't enough. "The trappers will come here to rescue the woman and to get the pelts back in their possession," he said tightly. "But we will not allow either to happen. We will have sentries close at all times, waiting for the evil men who caused the death of our two braves. They will not get past our warriors."

Mia had sat stiffly listening to all that he said and now truly felt like a captive. She hoped that when they were alone, he would show his caring, gentle side to her again. As he addressed his people now, he seemed a strong leader who was interested only in their well-being, not hers.

Mia now felt a new fear. Perhaps he had only been kind to her earlier because he wanted her to go with him without fighting and clawing to keep from being taken captive.

Perhaps she had made a mistake by accompanying him without a fight. She had only spoken angrily to him. Nothing more.

But now that she was a captive in his village, she had no choice but to hope that he would treat her fairly. She had done nothing to warrant poor treatment. It was up to her now to prove this to Wolf Hawk and his people.

And she would!

Somehow, she would.

"I will now take the woman to the lodge that is kept ready for lodging visitors," Wolf Hawk said blandly. "She will be guarded well."

Those words caused Mia's insides to turn cold.

Hearing that she would be guarded made her realize that she truly was a prisoner, and she could not help being afraid.

Yet she remembered just how gently this young chief had treated her and allowed herself to see hope in that.

When he rode onward through the large village, the children again began laughing and playing, seemingly having forgotten the stranger who had been brought into their midst. She was ignored by the adults of this tight-knit Indian community. The women and men were now going about their usual chores, while an older group of men, whom she thought were probably the elders of this band, sat in a huddle exchanging gossip and smokes from their long-stemmed pipes.

It was a peaceful scene, unlike anything that Mia had ever seen before. Everyone seemed to be happy with one another, as though they were all one big happy family.

Then as Wolf Hawk rode up to the large tepee that she now felt would be her "jail," she smelled food roasting over a fire.

She only now realized that she had not yet eaten today. The scent of the food made her stomach growl.

Wolf Hawk drew rein before the community house and dismounted.

He lifted his arms upward and placed his hands gently at Mia's waist. As she peered into his eyes with a bitterness he did not want her to feel, he attempted to distract her from dwelling on the fact that she was a captive among people so unlike her own.

"Food will be brought soon," he said as he lowered her to the ground.

The feel of her tininess in his hands made him reluctant to let her go. He knew he was wrong to allow himself such feelings about her.

But how could he not? She was one of the prettiest women he had ever seen, and when she was not being bitter and combative, her eyes seemed to express the sweetness he believed was in her heart.

She was not the sort who seemed to live her life with anger and mistrust.

When Mia heard that food would be brought, she wanted to lash out and say that she wished to have nothing cooked by his people, that she would rather starve. But the truth was that she needed nourishment in order to keep up her strength.

She would escape at her first opportunity, yet . . . where would she go? From whom would she seek help? She was alone, totally alone in the world.

She didn't respond to him, for she was afraid her words would hold too much bitterness in them. Instead she smiled sweetly and followed him inside the huge tepee.

She was stunned at its neat and comfortable appearance. The floors were covered with soft-looking mats, made from what looked like some sort of vines.

There was a fire burning in a fire pit circled by

rocks in the center of the lodge. The smoke from it spiraled slowly upward through a smoke hole.

Blankets and pelts were rolled up along the inside walls, having been put there for the visitor's comfort. Mia smiled at the sight. Her rear end felt numb after riding on the horse for so long, and she was looking forward to sitting on something soft.

Wolf Hawk seemed to have the ability to read her mind. He spread out a blanket, topped with a plush pelt, then gestured with a hand toward it.

"Sit," Wolf Hawk invited. "Get comfortable. I shall go for food."

He walked away, then stopped before going out through the entrance flap. "Do not attempt to leave, for even as I speak, a warrior stands guard outside the lodge," he said sternly.

He saw her eyes waver, and then she looked away from him.

He went outside and strode to the lodge of his cousin Little Snowbird, where he knew good food was always bubbling over the cook fire.

Little Snowbird smiled at him. "You are here to eat?" she asked. He ate most of his meals with her, especially since she had become a widow.

"I am here to take food to the white woman," Wolf Hawk said, hesitating at calling Mia a captive.

In his heart she was nothing of the kind. She was a woman he desired more each time he looked at her.

She had a way of reaching inside his heart and making him believe that she did not hate him.

He had seen her gaze at him more than once with the eyes of a woman who was interested in a certain man.

He was glad that she had given him that look, for he hoped to find her innocent of wrongdoing so that he could treat her as someone special . . . as someone he might ask to remain permanently in his village.

Since her father's death, she had no one to defend her or care for her. He felt the urge to become her protector.

In time he would know if his feelings toward her were warranted.

"Wolf Hawk, my cousin, do not let your eyes linger on that woman," Little Snowbird said, giving him a sideways glance as she prepared a platter to take to the woman. "She is not of our world, Wolf Hawk. Remember that. She . . . is . . . a part of the white race that has wronged so many of our people."

"You forget who you are talking to?" Wolf Hawk growled out. "Little Snowbird, I make my own decisions about things and I never enter into anything without being certain of what I do."

Little Snowbird gave him a sheepish look, then smiled as she handed the platter to Wolf Hawk. "It is because I love you too much," she murmured. "Ever since your mother left us to walk the road of the hereafter, I have become your mother."

"And I have appreciated your love and concern," Wolf Hawk said, taking the wooden tray from her. "I am sorry for having just spoken to you in a tone that is not usual for me. But know that I must be in control of my own heart. I guard it well."

"I know," Little Snowbird said. She reached up and patted him gently on his handsome, copper face. "I know. Go now. There is enough food for both you and the woman."

"And you would give me permission to eat with her?" Wolf Hawk said in a teasing fashion, his eyes gleaming playfully.

"Cousin, go," Little Snowbird said, taking him gently by the elbow and ushering him outside. "Enjoy the honey that I have placed with the venison to make it especially delicious."

"And you did this for the white captive?" Wolf Hawk asked, turning and smiling again mischievously at his cousin.

"I did it for you, not her," Little Snowbird said, lifting her chin stubbornly.

Then she laughed softly. "Go now or I shall take it away from you and eat it myself," she said, giving him a gentle shove toward the open flap.

Wolf Hawk laughed softly, too.

He left her tepee and walked toward the larger one, wondering just where his attraction for the white woman would end.

Chapter Fourteen

Light, so low upon earth,
You send a flash to the sun,
Here is the golden close of love.
All my wooing is done.
                    —*Alfred, Lord Tennyson*

As Mia waited for Wolf Hawk's return to the large tepee, she felt strangely anxious for his return.

Wolf Hawk was a man of much charisma and kindness, and although she was in his village as his captive, somehow she didn't feel like a prisoner, at all. He had treated her too gently, too caringly, for that.

As she sat there on the thick, soft pallet of furs and blankets, with the fire warm on her face, she saw that this tepee was vastly different from any dwelling that she had ever seen before. But she found it delightful to relax without feeling the sway of a boat beneath her or the fishy smell that surrounded her during the weeks of traveling with her parents each year.

She would never understand why her parents had preferred those times on the river, instead of living, year-round, in their St. Louis home, where they had such comforts.

Her father had tried to explain it by saying that while they were traveling on their scow, they were not dependant on anyone but themselves and that was the way they liked it.

She knew that they had decided to give up their river travel only because of her father's questionable health. How she wished that they had made that decision earlier. She truly believed that the hard work of steering the scow had helped weaken her father's heart.

She forced her mind away from the sadness of their deaths and again studied the lodge that would be her home for she knew not how long. Forever?

Or would she be set free as soon as the Indians learned that she was not guilty of any crimes against them? How would she survive in a world where she would be all alone and without family?

Again she forced her mind on to other things. Everything in this tepee smelled fresh and clean. The blankets and pelts rolled up against the walls, the mats on which she sat, were all that she would need to be comfortable while staying there. She could see why an Indian woman could be content in such a dwelling as this, especially if she had her family with her.

The thought of family brought instant tears to her eyes again, for she just could not stop thinking about the loss of her parents. She still could hardly believe the terrible changes in her world. Of course she had tried to prepare herself for her father's death since his health had been failing for some time, but the actuality of it was too much to bear.

After her mother's death, the knowledge that her father could leave her, too, had been so painful, that oft times she would get up in the middle of the night just to check on him, to see that he was still breathing.

In truth, she should not completely blame Wolf Hawk for her father's passing. Harry Collins had been dying long before he set eyes on the Winnebago chief. At least now he was no longer in pain.

She truly had no idea just how much he had suffered, but she knew he suffered no more. He lay with his eyes peacefully closed.

She would not think about him being in that shallow grave. In truth, he was with her mother, his precious wife. They were now together for eternity.

Her papa was with his beloved Glenna!

Mia had been caught up in such deep thoughts, she had not heard Wolf Hawk enter the lodge.

He stepped just inside the tepee and saw that she was lost in thought, gazing into the dancing flames of the fire.

He could only guess that she was thinking about her father, for her thoughts seemed intense. And he even heard a soft sob and saw her body tremble as if she were crying.

He was not certain whether he should leave her with her thoughts, or interrupt them and distract her with talk and food.

He had brought delicious things to eat. His cousin had prepared the best venison and had added to it a small portion of honey to make it even more tasty.

He knew that it surely had been some time since Mia had eaten, as it had been for himself, so he walked on into the tepee. The sound of his footsteps caused her to turn her eyes to him.

She wiped at her tears, yet said nothing to him.

But she did notice the offering of food and he believed he saw a glimmer of interest in her eyes. He surmised that she was as hungry as himself.

"My cousin has prepared us food," Wolf Hawk said, setting the tray beside Mia. "It has been awhile since I have eaten so I shall eat with you unless you would rather I didn't."

Mia was surprised that he would even give her a say in the matter. She was his captive. He could do anything he wanted, yet he was treating her gently and with respect.

More and more she saw the sort of man he truly was. He was ever so gentle and considerate. Surely it was because he remembered the loss of her loved ones and understood the grief she held so deep inside her heart.

"Yes, please stay," Mia murmured.

She gazed into his midnight-dark eyes and was shaken by the way they made her feel.

She had never felt anything for a man before. She had spent more time with her family than socializing with others.

"During my recent hunt, I searched for a bee's

nest where I could find honey for my widowed cousin. She prepares all my meals, and she sent some of this honey today to eat with the venison," he explained.

He held out the platter, encouraging her to take food from it since she still hesitated to do so.

"Take a piece of meat, then dip it into the honey," he softly urged. "You will soon realize how good it is."

"I have never eaten meat with honey," Mia said, plucking a strip of the meat from the tray.

"Dip it," Wolf Hawk said, nodding toward her.

He watched her as she finally did dip the venison into the honey.

He waited anxiously for her reaction.

He smiled when he saw from the expression in her eyes that she liked it.

He understood now the wisdom of putting the honey with the meat. His cousin had realized that a young lady who had been taken captive by Indians needed something to lessen her fear of being with them.

And she knew that the sweetness of honey could reach into anyone's heart and make a person feel more relaxed.

"It is very good," Mia said, surprised and now eager to take another bite. She hesitated, however, for Wolf Hawk had not eaten any of it yet.

Hungry, and now satisfied that he had pleased the woman, Wolf Hawk set the tray down, then took his own piece of meat and dipped it into the honey.

He ate it eagerly, smiling to himself when Mia no longer hesitated, but now ate bite after bite of venison dripping in honey.

"I am glad that you are enjoying the meat. The best meal is one that is shared with friends," Wolf Hawk said, feeling pleasantly full. He sat more comfortably with his legs crossed before him, his hands resting on his knees.

"I take pride in being a good hunter," he said, smiling at Mia. "And a good chief. I share what I bring home from the hunt with those of our clan who have no father, brother or husband to hunt for them. No one goes hungry in the village of Wolf Hawk."

"If you are a hunter, does that not mean that you trap animals just like the white men you wish to find and punish?" Mia dared to ask.

"We do trap small game," Wolf Hawk admitted. "But we have never used traps that have steel jaws, which cause the animals so much suffering."

"Then what sort do you use?" Mia asked. "Isn't one trap as deadly as another?"

"My warrior hunters use traps that kill instantly," Wolf Hawk explained. "Ours do not maim and leave the animals to die slowly."

"But how can you be certain?" Mia prodded, feeling that one trap was as bad as the next.

"I will explain and then you will understand that our way is humane while the white man's steel traps are not," Wolf Hawk said. "And our traps would never catch humans in them as the trappers' did."

"I'm certain they did not mean to kill the braves," Mia murmured.

Wolf Hawk's insides tightened. "You are defending the trappers?" he asked thickly. "Perhaps you really do know them and approve of what they are guilty of having done?"

Mia gasped at what he was implying. That was the last thing she wanted Wolf Hawk to think!

"I am not defending them, for I think what they did was horrible, and, no, I do not know them," she blurted out, her face hot with a nervous flush that she wished wasn't there.

She had to prove to this Indian that she was innocent of the trappers' crimes and that she did not know them. She also had to be more careful what she said to him. Her life might depend on it.

"I hope that what you speak is truth, for I am beginning to trust that you are what you say you are," Wolf Hawk told her. "I am my people's leader. They depend on me to choose the right path. I have seen much innocence in you, and loneliness. You have known deep sorrow at the loss of your parents, and now you are alone. Remember this . . . if you wish to allow me to help fill that lonely space inside you, I would be happy to."

"But . . . I . . . am your captive," Mia blurted out, stunned at his suggestion. "How can you help me feel less lonely? Why should you care?"

Wolf Hawk wanted badly to reach out and touch her face, which had become flushed. "Just trust that I do care and I will not allow any harm to come your way while you are with me and my people. Did I not feed you well? Are you not in a safe place with comforts all around you? Is not the fire warm against your flesh?"

"Yes, you did all of those things for me, yet . . . I . . . am still a captive," Mia said, slowly lowering her eyes. "That word . . . captive. It fills me with dread."

He reached over and dared to place his hand beneath her chin. Slowly he lifted it so that her eyes were level with his.

"You are not a true captive," he said, surprising himself that he would admit such a thing to her.

But he was now sure that she had had nothing to do with the evil men he hunted.

"If I am not a true captive, why not let me go now and allow me to find my own way in the world?" Mia said, all the while fearing that he just might take her up on the suggestion.

If so, where would she go?

Who would she ask for help?

While here with Wolf Hawk, she at least felt safe, for she now knew that he would never harm her. She could sense that he had feelings for her, just as she did for him.

When she sat with him, it was easy not to see him as an Indian, but instead, a very handsome man who was treating her ever so gently!

"It is too soon for you to be thrust out into this cruel world, alone," Wolf Hawk said, searching her eyes. "I promise you, white woman, that while you are with me, no harm will come to you. But once you are out in the world, you will have no one to watch over you."

"Why would you care?" Mia asked, now searching his dark eyes and seeing emotions that surely he would not say aloud.

"I will continue telling you about the way my warriors trap animals when they hunt," Wolf Hawk blurted out. He felt a need to change the subject, which was becoming much too personal.

He had to wait and make certain that his feelings for this woman were real.

"Yes, please tell me," Mia murmured. "I would truly like to know. The steel traps are so inhumane. I have always thought they should not be allowed. But there are a lot of things that are wrong, yet used. I am glad to know that you have chosen a more decent way to trap the animals that you need for your people's survival."

"Yes, it is for our survival," Wolf Hawk said thickly. "Once you hear, though, you will see that our way is definitely the best way."

"Please do tell me," Mia murmured, feeling more comfortable with him by the minute.

"My men build the trap by propping up a heavy log on a pole. The bait is tied to the pole," Wolf Hawk said. "As soon as the animal touches the bait, the heavy log falls on its head. It is killed instantly. There is no suffering."

He realized just as soon as he said it that even his people's way of trapping did not lessen the sadness in Mia's heart at the killing of animals.

She was a gentle, caring woman, who preferred to take in animals and care for them, not kill them.

"I see that what I said still offends you," he observed, his voice drawn. "I apologize for that. Perhaps sometime you had an animal that you kept as a pet?"

She was catapulted back to the moment she'd found Georgina's empty cage this morning. Her hatred for Tiny multiplied inside her heart every time she thought about how he had allowed her canary to fly free of its cage.

"Yes, I had a pet," she said, her voice catching with emotion.

Tears flooded her eyes as she wondered where Georgina was now? Was she all alone in the forest . . . or dead?

Mia truly feared the little bird had been killed.

"It was what sort of a pet?" Wolf Hawk asked.

"A bird," she murmured, brushing tears from her cheeks with the back of a hand.

"You captured a bird and kept it as a pet?" Wolf Hawk asked, his eyebrows lifting. He could not envision any bird staying with him, tamed enough not to fly away at its first opportunity. His connection with hawks made all birds seem sacred in his eyes.

"No, I did not capture it," Mia said, smiling through her tears. "I purchased it from someone at a trading post."

"I have never seen birds being sold at a trading post," Wolf Hawk said, truly curious now.

"It is not just any ordinary bird that might fly free in the forest," Mia tried to explain. She was charmed that he did not know of such things.

"It was a canary," she said. "A canary is a tiny yellow bird raised to be a pet. It is not only beautiful, a joy to be with, but it also sings melodies all day long."

"Birds usually sing because they are happy," Wolf Hawk said. "Does that mean that your bird was happy to be in a cage?"

"It knew nothing else," Mia murmured. "And, yes, she was happy. I gave her food and clean water every day. She loved me as much as I loved her."

"And where is your bird now?" Wolf Hawk asked softly.

"Tiny released her to the wild," Mia blurted out, anger flashing in her eyes. She knew he had done it on purpose to hurt her.

"The tiny man that refused to help you dig the grave for your father?" Wolf Hawk asked softly.

"Yes, him," Mia said, her voice breaking with emotion as she envisioned Georgina so afraid, so alone!

She hoped her precious canary was still alive to have those feelings, for it would be better than being caught in the claws of a hawk and eaten.

"Why would he do that?" Wolf Hawk asked, leaning closer to Mia until their faces were only inches apart.

"To spite me," Mia said, oh, so aware of how close Wolf Hawk was to her.

Their lips were only a breath apart.

She had never ached to be kissed before, but now?

She did!

And she recalled the strength of his arms as he had swept them around her to lift her onto his horse. She remembered the clean, fresh smell of his skin and hair. She remembered the new feeling of passion he evoked within her.

"Why would he want to spite you?" Wolf Hawk asked, daringly reaching a hand to her cheek and gently touching it. He drew it away when he saw how wide her eyes grew over what he had just done.

"Because he was the sort of man who enjoyed causing other people pain, and losing my bird hurt me very much," Mia murmured.

Her heart was thumping hard inside her chest over the way Wolf Hawk had touched her face so gently, so lovingly.

Everything within her cried out to be held tenderly in his arms. She wanted him never to let her go, for she feared what lay ahead of her; she feared being totally alone in the world.

"Our search for this man was unsuccessful," Wolf Hawk said thickly. "He is so small, he could find a lot of places to hide where no one would see him."

"He will probably flag down someone traveling by on the river and go on his way, and I say good riddance to bad rubbish," Mia said sourly.

"What is this saying . . . good riddance to bad

rubbish . . . ?" Wolf Hawk asked, raising his eyebrows.

Mia laughed softly at his question. "It is a way of saying that I am glad Tiny is gone and I hope I never see him again."

Chapter Fifteen

I have heard of thorns and briers,
Over the meadow and stiles,
Over the world to the end of it,
Flash for a million mile—
                              —Alfred, Lord Tennyson

Breathless with fear, Tiny scrambled back through the gates of the fort. He couldn't believe that he had successfully eluded the redskin savages, but he had, by climbing high into a tree and crouching amid the thick foliage.

Even if the warriors had looked up and tried to peer through the leaves, they couldn't have seen him. He had clung to the tree while the Indians rode past below him.

He smiled at his cleverness. He had often hidden in a tree when he and his three brothers and one sister had played games of hide-and-seek. No one could find him until they finally learned that he would always use that trick.

Once he had been found out, the game was over for him. He had never successfully hidden himself again.

That was when he learned tricks with cards, for that was another way to best his brothers and sister. He never wanted to lose at anything. He had become so skilled at cards that he won much money after leaving home and becoming a successful gambler.

But even in that he was discovered and almost lost his life one night at a tavern after cheating a burly, unkempt man out of all of his money.

The man had held Tiny upside down by his heels, shaking the money he had wrongly won from his breeches pocket. After that Tiny was careful whom he gambled with. The itch was too strong to ever quit completely!

With dusk quickly shadowing everything around Tiny, he hurried inside the cabin where he had stayed with Mia and her father. He felt safe inside the fort now, at least for awhile. He doubted the Indians would return.

He had seen the mound of earth beneath the trees outside of the fort's walls. Harry's grave. Yep, that was where Harry lay, unable to order Tiny around any longer.

"You earned what you got," Tiny said, snickering. He looked around him. He was glad to have a decent enough place to stay until tomorrow, when he would get as far from this danged place as possible.

He went to the supplies that Mia had left behind. He found some crusty bread. He smiled when he saw the jar of strawberry jam that Mia's mother had made back in St. Louis.

He unscrewed the lid and poked a finger into it, dug some jam out with his finger, and spread it quickly across the bread even though the edges were moldy.

His belly ached from hunger.

He had to get as much nourishment as he could, for he had no idea when he might be able to eat again.

He was hoping to find a boat that would take him to St. Louis. He had cousins there. They would take him in.

The problem was that he had not seen hide nor hair of anyone on the river since several days ago. If no one came along in the morning, he would have to start walking, hoping to find the home of some settler who might offer him a comfortable night's lodging and decent food.

Then he'd ask for help getting to a town, and he'd find his way on to good ol' Saint Louie, hisself!

Enjoying the strawberry taste of the jam as long as he could, Tiny stepped from the cabin and gazed toward the opened gate of the fort. He knew that he didn't have much more time before it got dark. At dawn tomorrow he'd leave this place once and for all.

He started to close the gate, to keep undesirable critters from coming inside, but then he realized that the Indians might notice that the position of the gate had changed.

"Best leave it be," he whispered to himself.

He went back inside the cabin.

He stopped and eyed that door.

It had been left ajar, too, so he decided not to close it completely, either.

"I guess I'll have to sleep tonight chancing that some wild thing might come along and mosey inside with me," he mumbled to himself.

He knew, though, that he would rather take that risk than possibly alert Indians to his presence.

The cabin was growing chilly as darkness dropped around it. He turned and eyed the fireplace and the wood that was stacked beside it. Oh, how he would love the warmth of that fire through the night. Yet again, he had to out think the savages and knew that smoke would draw them there.

He saw blankets lying on the floor where Harry had spent the night. He shuddered at resting in a place where a dead man had slept.

But Harry hadn't died in those blankets.

So tired he could hardly keep his eyes open any longer, he lay down on the blankets, but sleep eluded him as the moon sent its light down through a window and onto his face.

"If it ain't one thing, it's another," he growled.

He yanked his cards out of his rear breeches pocket, finding it strange that they were all he had left of his worldly possessions.

He shuffled them, dealt himself a hand of poker, then dealt another to a pretend person in front of him. He played both hands, snickering when, of course, he was the winner again.

"I can't even beat myself," he said, laughing throatily.

He slid the cards aside on the floor, then yawning, he stretched out again on the blankets. Feeling cold, he yanked one of the blankets from beneath him and pulled it snugly around himself.

He fell into a restless sleep and was awakened suddenly in the night by something sniffing at his face. When he opened his eyes, he stiffened with intense fear when he found a wolf there, gazing at him directly in the eyes.

Tiny let out a loud shriek, which startled the wolf. Tiny watched it make a wide, quick turn and run from the cabin.

"Well, that's enough of that," he whispered to himself. "I'm gettin' outta here while the gettin' is good."

But he would never forget coming eye to eye with a wolf and livin' to eventually tell someone about it.

He gathered up his cards, stuffed them in his rear pocket, and ran from the cabin. He fled the fort, and kept running, hoping the wolf wasn't following his scent.

Tiny stumbled through the forest, not realizing that he was going farther and farther from the river.

Suddenly he tripped and fell hard to the ground.

He was unaware of his cards flying from his pocket, or the wind taking them up and blowing each in a different direction.

Chapter Sixteen

In life we share a single guilt,
In death we will share a single coffin.
                                        —*Tao-Sheng*

The mournful sounds of people wailing, of flutes
and drums being played, filled the village of the
Bird Clan.

Wolf Hawk had come to Mia at daybreak and
awakened her. He had carried a tray of fruits and
meats, and she'd been surprised that he would
awaken her so early to eat the morning meal.

But moments later she understood.

He had told her that today his people would
hold the burial rites for the two fallen braves. He
had said that he would be gone for most of the day,
joining the rites.

He also had told her that no warrior would be
standing outside her appointed lodge, for all the
people of his village would be participating.

He had told her that he trusted her not to flee
now that she knew she was in no danger of being
harmed while she was among his people. Oddly
enough he had not asked her to promise not to
escape.

She hated the idea of leaving after looking into

his midnight-dark eyes. There was not only trust in them, but also caring.

She did not know how it could be happening, but she, too, cared for him. It was his voice, his manner, his magical way of just being who he was, so handsome and intriguing, that had awoken these feelings that she had never felt for a man before.

And she no longer blamed him for her father's death. She knew that her father had been living on borrowed time. His heart had been steadily weakening all during their trip.

"Oh, Papa, I miss you so," Mia sobbed out, feeling an emptiness inside at the thought of never seeing him or being held by him again.

All that she had ever known was gone now.

It was only herself, and . . .

No. She should not put Wolf Hawk into the category of someone who was now a part of her world, for she knew that he would soon set her free to go on her way, to find her way alone in the world. She should not put aside her plans for him.

Wolf Hawk was just someone taking a role in her life for a short while, and then, he, too, would be in her past. Although they both obviously had feelings for each other, he was a proud chief, and he would surely not make a white woman a permanent part of his world.

"What am I to do?" Mia said, standing and pacing.

She had eaten and felt comfortably full.

The morning air was now warm and pleasant

as it wafted through the opened entrance flap, which she had brushed aside.

There was a soft fire in the fire pit, which she planned to let burn itself out. The sun was shining so bright today, she believed it was going to be one of the warmer days of spring.

"A good day to flee . . ." she found herself whispering.

She stepped to the entranceway and gazed out. She saw no one. The procession of Wolf Hawk's people had left the village, and must have reached their burial grounds with the two fallen youths.

She had seen them being carried on two travois behind powerfully muscled horses. The bodies had been wrapped in blankets so that their faces were not visible.

But their belongings lay on each side of them, with some hanging from thin poles that had been attached to the travois. There was a drum, a pair of moccasins, and several feathers tied in a bundle.

There were more things, but she had felt they were too sad to look at. She imagined those things were to be buried with the boys. Probably they were the braves' most precious possessions.

She choked on a sob to think of her father all alone beneath that mound of dirt. She had not even thought to bury something of his with him, as these Indians were doing.

But his most precious possession had been his pipe, and that now lay at the bottom of the river.

"I should have buried his book of poetry with

him," she whispered, gazing at it where it lay with her mother's Bible.

She would have to leave them and all her other belongings behind, for she would have to move with speed, and could not carry anything that would slow her down.

She knew that once the burial rites were over, Wolf Hawk would come to the lodge and find her gone. She wondered how angry he would be.

Or would he be hurt? Would he feel that she had betrayed his trust?

"No matter which, I must go," she said aloud, her decision suddenly final.

Yes, she trusted Wolf Hawk never to harm her, but she was not so sure about the other members of the village. They did not feel the same kindness toward her that Wolf Hawk felt.

She was afraid that as soon as the burial of the two fallen youths was over, these people would center their attention on her. They would hold her to blame for the boys' deaths.

She had no choice but to leave.

Her heart pounding, she slowly crept from the large tepee. She looked from side to side to see if Wolf Hawk had told the truth about her being left unguarded, and found that it was so.

She saw no one, though she could still hear the flute and drums and wailing, which now came from somewhere deep in the forest. She would have to make certain to go in the opposite direction from those sounds.

She gazed at her travel bag, in which were all of

her belongings. She hated leaving them behind, but anything she would carry would burden her down too much.

She would have to depend on the goodness of others once she got away from the village. She would search for a settler's home where she might take shelter.

If she didn't find a home, then she would have to make her way back to the river and hope that someone would come along and take her with them.

One way or another she would find a way back to St. Louis where her parents' home stood silent, cold and empty.

Her pulse racing, her face flushed, her hair tied back into a ponytail to keep it from getting in her way, she ran around to the back of the large tepee, then sped on into the darkest shadows of the forest.

She made certain she did not go toward that part of the forest where the burial rites were being held. She had watched which way the people had gone, and she felt safe that she would not be seen.

The part of her that was enamored with Wolf Hawk ached, for she hated the thought that she would never see him or hear his voice again.

She had loved his gentleness toward her. But he would not be gentle now, not when she had betrayed his trust, throwing away any chance of getting to know Wolf Hawk better.

She grew breathless as she ran onward through the dense forest.

She felt a deep sadness when she heard the songs of the birds floating like beautiful silk through the air, reminding her of her lost canary.

Georgina.

Oh, where was her sweet Georgina? Mia doubted that Georgina was still alive and that hurt her deeply and made her hate Tiny. She hoped she would never see that man again.

She tried to focus on something besides her anger toward Tiny, her loneliness without her family and her bird. Instead, she concentrated on the beauty of her surroundings.

She could smell the wondrous scent of wild roses coming from somewhere in amongst the trees.

Oft times she had seen them climbing up the trunks of trees when her father had stopped the scow for their nightly layovers. She had picked a bouquet for her mother more than once.

Her mother had loved lily of the valley, too, which Mia could also smell though she could not see the tiny plant with its even tinier white flowers.

Its sweet fragrance reminded her so much of her mother. She had seen her mother pluck these flowers and put several in her hair, laughing softly as she said she wore a crown, and wasn't it ever so beautiful and sweet?

Mia also saw clover dotting the forest floor and recalled how her mother had made her a chain bracelet of them.

It was the simple things she remembered her mother doing that made Mia miss her so terribly.

As she fled farther and farther into the forest, Mia no longer heard the wailing or the flute or drums. She must have traveled far from the Winnebago village. That meant she was also far from the man she would never forget . . . his gentleness, his caring, his eyes.

Oh, how his eyes sent her heart into a spin.

How could she have left, knowing she would never experience such feelings again?

There could be no one else like him, and yet she had left Wolf Hawk, never to marvel over his sweet kindness again.

She raised her chin and made herself stop thinking what she knew was wrong.

She had to find a way to fend for herself in this heartless, lonely world. And she would.

Her papa had taught her to stand up for herself. She would not let him down.

Suddenly she stopped. Her eyes filled with dismay.

While she was thinking so hard about other things, she had not watched where she was going. She had walked right into the middle of thick poison ivy vines. The leaves were even up the inside of her skirt, touching the bare flesh of her legs.

She already felt her skin itch, for she had learned long ago that she got poison ivy immediately and became very ill from it before getting better.

She had had such a severe reaction at times that she had thought she might die.

"Oh, Lord, what have I done?" she cried as she looked around herself.

The vines were everywhere. They were climbing up the trunks of the trees, overpowering everything within reach.

They covered the ground so thickly, there was no way she could get free of the tangle without the leaves touching the skin of her legs over and over again.

Mia now realized how wrong she had been to flee the Indian village. She was without protection of any kind out here in the wild.

What if she grew as ill from the poison ivy this time as she had the last, and she was all alone, with no one to care for her?

"I must go back," she whispered, as tears spilled from her eyes. "I must!"

She truly had no choice.

She cringed with each step she took as the shiny, three-pointed leaves brushed against her skin. Her legs were already itching and hurting her.

When she got poison ivy, it was not just a few bumps on her flesh. In the past her legs had swollen to double their normal size.

Breaking into a wet sweat all over her body, Mia began to run. Half an hour later, she was never so glad to see anything as when she spotted tepees through a break in the trees a short distance away.

Suddenly she stopped. Up ahead, near the first of the tepees of the village, she saw a strange mist moving toward the dwellings.

She gasped and felt faint when she saw the mist coalesce and take on the form of Wolf Hawk, who now ran on toward his own lodge, which was set some distance from the other tepees.

"What does it mean?" Mia whispered to herself, shaken by what she had seen. How could the young chief have materialized from the hazy mist?

She was glad that he had not seen her, for she was well hidden in the dark shadows of the forest. She felt it was best that he wasn't aware of what she had seen.

It seemed so fantastic, she wondered if the event was just a figment of her imagination.

Yes, that's what it was, she told herself. It hadn't been real at all.

She had imagined seeing the mist. Probably, she was so anxious about the poison ivy making her ill that her mind was playing tricks on her.

Trembling, unable to truly make herself believe that what she had seen had not been real, she hurried on into the village and went to the tepee where she had been staying.

Once inside, she hurried over to what was left of the fire. She was cold inside and out from everything that had just happened to her.

And she was so afraid of how sick she might become from the poison ivy, she wasn't sure what to do.

She hated the idea of asking the aid of an Indian Shaman. She wouldn't do it until she knew that she must. She would wait and see how bad the poison ivy got.

She jerked with alarm when Wolf Hawk came suddenly into the tepee.

She turned slowly and gazed into his eyes, seeing that he knew something was wrong. There was a questioning look on his face.

Wolf Hawk saw how Mia was trembling, and he saw telltale signs that she had been in the forest, for there were pieces of grass and leaves snagged on the skirt of her dress.

He again gazed deeply into her eyes. He knew now that while he was gone she had decided to go into the forest, but why?

Had she planned to flee, yet changed her mind? Had something frightened her into returning to the safety of his people's village?

Needing answers, he stepped closer to her and reached a hand out for her.

When she winced and drew quickly away from him, with a look of fear in her eyes, he was stunned.

"Why are you behaving so strangely?" he asked, searching her face. "You are trembling, yet the lodge is not cold. Are you ill?"

She shoved him away.

"Why would you do that?" he asked, taking a step back.

He knew that something was terribly wrong and yet she would not confide in him what it was.

"Please leave me alone," Mia blurted out. In her mind's eye she again saw the mist, and Wolf Hawk appearing out of thin air.

In her mind's eye she also saw the poison ivy

reaching out for her like devil fingers, ready to kill her if it could!

"You wish to be alone . . . you shall get that wish," Wolf Hawk said tightly, then turned and left. The clean, fresh smell of his hair and his body wafted through the air behind him. Mia inhaled it and imagined him, holding her, embracing her, loving her.

Tears filled her eyes.

She fell to her knees beside the fire and held her face in her hands.

Suddenly everything was so confusing. She feared what tomorrow would bring.

Chapter Seventeen

I prithee send me back my heart,
Since I cannot have thine;
For if from yours you will not part,
Why then shoulds't thou have mine?
                              —Sir John Suckling

Even before she was awake, Mia groaned with discomfort. Then she opened her eyes and cried out in despair when she saw just how bad her poison ivy was.

She threw aside the blanket she had slept under. It felt damp and clammy.

She sat up and gasped. By the moonlight that came down from the smoke hole above, she saw just how bad the poison ivy on her legs was. They were swollen to twice their normal size, and the itching sores were seeping fluid, which had gotten the blanket wet.

"Oh, what am I to do?" she cried softly.

She knew that if the poison ivy wasn't medicated soon, and in the right way, she might even lose her legs. A friend of her father had gotten poison ivy and lost an arm because of it, mainly because he had not taken it seriously enough to go to a doctor when he should have.

But Mia had no idea where the nearest town

might be or if it even had a doctor who could help her.

The itching and hurting was almost driving her wild, yet she knew that scratching the rash would only make it worse. Mia lay back down and sobbed so hard, her body shook.

When Wolf Hawk spoke her name outside the closed entrance flap, her eyes widened.

She hadn't seen him since she had asked him to leave her tepee.

"Come in," she said weakly.

She wiped the tears from her eyes and cheeks with the palm of a hand.

She gazed again at her seeping legs, which she just could not cover again with a blanket. It would cause her even more pain if the blanket were to make contact with her sores.

She then looked up at Wolf Hawk as he came into the tepee with a tray of food for her dinner.

When he saw her and how ill she was from the poison ivy, he almost dropped the tray in shock.

He knew what was ailing her.

He had seen this kind of rash before on the legs of the children who had gone farther into the forest than was usually allowed and got entangled in the poison vine. Some of them had become very ill because of it.

They had even lost one child whose body had been too weak to fight off the horrible effects of the poison vine. Even his grandfather Shaman had not been able to stop the child from dying.

He looked more closely at Mia's legs, worried

when he saw just how badly she was afflicted by the poison of the vine. Were she to die, he would always blame himself for having brought her to his village. Why had she felt the need to flee his people even though she had not been mistreated?

But he understood. She saw herself as a captive, and the very word was enough to send dread into anyone's heart.

He wished now that he had told her he saw her not as a captive, but instead as a woman he had deep feelings for.

And now?

No sooner had he found a woman who affected his heart in such a sensuous way, than he feared he might lose her.

"I must get you to Shadow Island," he exclaimed, already setting the tray on the floor. "Now. Not later."

"Shadow Island?" Mia asked meekly, still nervous of Wolf Hawk after seeing him appear in such a mysterious way yesterday.

But she couldn't ask him about what she had seen. She was afraid of what his reaction would be.

"Shadow Island is where my grandfather Shaman lives," Wolf Hawk said.

He bent to his knees to sweep her into his arms, then stopped. He had never taken a white person to Shadow Island before, but now he must. He knew that he must get Mia to his grandfather and ask Talking Bird to use his magic cures on her. The woman was so ill. Talking Bird was her only chance of surviving this horrible sickness.

And Wolf Hawk was desperate for her to survive. He cared deeply for her.

He had hoped she would want to stay at his village, not flee from it, as he now knew she had tried to do yesterday. After she had asked him to leave the tepee, he had followed her tracks far from his village and straight into the poison vine area.

He knew that was why she had returned. She had surely had experience with the poison vine before and knew that she would have a bad reaction to it.

She had actually returned to plea for help; his.

"You are so kind to do this for me," Mia murmured as she felt his powerful arms lift her up.

"My grandfather knows all things," Wolf Hawk said as he carried her from the tepee, ignoring the surprised looks of his people, and hurried toward his canoe.

He would have preferred to fly her over to the island, but knew that seeing him in hawk form would terrify her. No. He had to keep her from discovering his mystical abilities.

He gazed into her eyes as she looked up at him while he gently laid her in the canoe. "My grandfather will make you well," he said, searching her eyes. He was glad to see trust in them. But there was something else, too. It was a look of wonder, as though she knew something that he didn't.

He was curious what that look meant, but he had no time to dwell on it now. He had to focus on getting her well. He did not want to lose her after having just found and fallen in love with her.

He had been attracted to many women of his tribe, yet none had spoken to his heart as had this woman.

He did not want to believe that his people would shun him were he to announce his feelings for this white woman. They knew him well and understood that he always acted out of the goodness of his heart.

Mia lay on the floor of the canoe as Wolf Hawk shoved it out into the water, then climbed aboard himself.

She began shivering, both from a fever that had just claimed her, and fear of what lay ahead. In the river she could see a small island that was partly obscured by mist.

Although her flesh was hot, she shivered with a chill that made her teeth chatter.

Aware that Mia was growing worse, Wolf Hawk drew the paddle more determinedly through the water, his eyes now focused on the island.

As it grew closer, he began to wonder what his grandfather would think about his bringing a white woman to Shadow Island. Never had he treated anyone with white skin before.

Would he think it wrong of Wolf Hawk to ask this of him? Or would he understand the feelings that Wolf Hawk had for the woman?

Almost delirious now with her fever, Mia whispered, "Papa . . . Mama . . . I shall soon join you."

Chapter Eighteen

The locked drops rising in a dew
Limpid as spirits.
Many stones lay dense and expressionless,
  Round about.
I didn't know what to make of it!
                                    —Sylvia Plath

As Wolf Hawk made his way toward Shadow Island, Mia subsided into a semiconscious state.

The splash of the water from his paddle made her believe that she was on the river with her family again, in their scow, happy and laughing together before her father's heart had become a problem and before Mia had grown tired of river travel.

The rocking of the boat lulled her into wonderful memories of being with her parents again, while occasional drops of water against her fevered brow felt cool and refreshing.

If she listened hard enough, she could actually hear her mother's sweet laughter and her father tapping his pipe empty of tobacco against the sides of the scow after finishing a lengthy smoke.

She could even smell the distinctive scent of of the tobacco he had used. It always reminded her of sweet apples in the autumn.

"We are at the island now," Wolf Hawk said, breaking into Mia's memories.

She opened her eyes, but she could barely see Wolf Hawk as he leapt over the side of the canoe. He waded through the shallow water, shoving the canoe onto the sandy shore.

He came to her and gazed into her eyes, concerned when he saw how bloodshot they were, and that she seemed hardly able to keep them open.

"You are going to be alright," Wolf Hawk quickly reassured her. He reached a gentle hand to her hot cheek, where her flesh was free of the terrible rash. "My grandfather Shaman will make it so."

"I . . . I . . . have never been . . . this . . . ill," Mia managed to say.

She was fighting to stay conscious. She wanted to be awake when the Shaman began working his magic on her. She wanted to be aware of what he did.

Although she trusted Wolf Hawk with every fiber of her being now, she still recalled how she had heard men laughing and calling Indian Shamans witch doctors who practiced voodoo on their people when they were ill.

"You will soon be well," Wolf Hawk said, gently lifting her from the canoe.

He was Mia's protector now, and he would make certain she allowed him to be the one who looked out for her and keep her safe from all harm, forevermore.

Mia drifted in and out of consciousness, but she was aware of Wolf Hawk's muscled arms as he lifted her gently from the canoe.

She was aware, too, that he was not walking as he carried her to his grandfather's home, but running. She knew that he was truly concerned about her, and wanted to get her help as soon as possible.

She could not help loving him for that. And as he carried her through a grove of wolf willows, which glowed eerily in the moonlight as a slow fog came creeping upon the land, she began to feel more comfortable about what was happening.

She did trust Wolf Hawk.

And she knew that whatever his grandfather Shaman might do in his effort to make her well, she would accept it.

At this moment in time, she had only Wolf Hawk as her protector. She now trusted him implicitly.

"Do not be afraid," Wolf Hawk said, knowing that all of this must be so strange to her. But this visit was completely necessary. If his grandfather did not use his magical cures on Mia, she might not live for many more tomorrows, and he wanted her with him forever, not only for a few more feverish days.

"I suddenly feel no fear," Mia murmured, then licked her dry, parched lips. "I . . . I . . . want to be well, Wolf Hawk."

"And you will be," Wolf Hawk replied.

He emerged on the other side of the wolf willows and now headed directly toward his grandfather's large tepee, which cast a huge shadow all around it as it sat in the bright moonlight.

"Mia, I promise that you will be well," Wolf Hawk again reassured her. "Soon."

"I . . . trust . . . you," Mia murmured. She again licked her parched lips. "I . . . even trust . . . your grandfather because he is your kin."

"Mia, you need trust and faith now more than ever before. You must feel both for my grandfather's magic to work on you," Wolf Hawk said, stopping right outside his grandfather's closed entrance flap.

"Magic?" Mia said, her eyes widening. "He is going to use magic to make me well?"

"Do not let that word bring fear back into your heart," Wolf Hawk said thickly. "Just think good things and good things will happen to you."

"I will," Mia said, watching now as Wolf Hawk spoke his grandfather's name.

Scarcely breathing, she waited and watched for the entrance flap to be drawn aside. When it was, she found herself gazing at the oldest person she had ever seen. The Shaman stood there in what looked like a bearskin robe, his gray hair worn in one long braid down his back.

He was a tiny man, much shorter than his grandson Wolf Hawk. He seemed to have shrunk from old age, and his face was furrowed with many wrinkles.

But in the moon's glow she saw eyes that did not show any signs of age. Instead they were dark and brilliant.

And as she gazed into them, she saw kindness, even wisdom. She felt that she was right not to fear him.

"Grandfather, this woman is in need of your curative powers," Wolf Hawk said, realizing immediately that his grandfather was hesitant to ask him and Mia into his lodge.

He understood.

No whites had ever been on this island, nor even in their village, which had purposely been established far from any white man's home.

And now? His grandson had actually brought one of the white eyes to his private island?

Ho, Yes, Wolf Hawk understood his grandfather's hesitance. But for the first time in his life, Wolf Hawk would prove his grandfather wrong about something.

He must, for the life of this woman Wolf Hawk cared so deeply for lay in the balance.

"Grandfather, this is a friend and she is in need of your help," Wolf Hawk said thickly.

"She is white," Talking Bird said flatly. "Her skin is the color of our enemy's."

"Although her skin is white, she is special to me," Wolf Hawk admitted. "And she is not our enemy. She is a friend, a friend who seeks help from someone who has the power to heal her."

Talking Bird continued to stand in his doorway,

blocking Wolf Hawk's entrance into his medicine lodge.

Slowly Wolf Hawk lowered Mia to the ground, laying her on a thick bed of moss that stretched out, like soft silk, around his grandfather's lodge. It had been purposely removed from the forest floor and planted there by Wolf Hawk for his grandfather's comfort.

Wolf Hawk gazed up at his grandfather. "I will show you," he said thickly.

Then Wolf Hawk gazed into Mia's eyes, which were once again filled with fear at the way she had been received by Wolf Hawk's Shaman grandfather.

She was white. She had a reason to be afraid.

It was up to Wolf Hawk to make both his grandfather and his woman feel more comfortable with each other so that Mia could be healed.

Wolf Hawk slowly lifted the hem of her dress to reveal Mia's swollen, seeping legs to his grandfather. "She found herself in the midst of poison vine and she is now ill from her reaction to it," he said, again gazing up at his grandfather.

He exhaled with relief when he saw the caring in his grandfather's eyes that Wolf Hawk was accustomed to.

His grandfather understood the urgency of Mia's condition. He would treat her, even though her skin was white. Wolf Hawk had been sure his grandfather would never have turned away someone who so desperately needed his help.

Talking Bird stepped aside and held the flap open so Wolf Hawk could enter. "Go inside," he said, his voice filled with true concern. "Take her with you. I will do what I can for the woman."

Mia sighed with relief.

She smiled up at the elderly man.

"Thank you," she murmured, oh, so glad that these Winnebago Indians knew the English language as well as they did. It made things much easier for her. "Thank you so much."

"My name is Talking Bird," the Shaman said, gently smiling now at Mia. "By what name are you called?"

"Mia," she murmured.

She felt again the wonder of Wolf Hawk's muscled arms as he swept her up from the beautifully soft moss.

She lay there trustingly in his arms as he carried her inside. Talking Bird followed and gestured with a frail hand toward several pelts that were spread out on the floor near the fire.

"I will see her better beside the fire," Talking Bird said. He gazed up at the smoke hole overhead, glad that the moon was as bright tonight as it was, for it, too, lent him more light by which to work his magic.

Wolf Hawk very gently laid Mia on the pelts, then stood back and rested himself on his haunches as his grandfather approached Mia and examined her legs more closely.

"My tobacco bag," Talking Bird said, glancing over at Wolf Hawk.

Understanding that his grandfather wished to offer tobacco to the spirits before he used his medicine on Mia, Wolf Hawk reached behind him and grabbed the drawstring pouch, then gave it to Talking Bird.

He sat down then, folded his legs before him, rested his hands on his knees and watched. He hoped that what his grandfather was going to do wouldn't bring fear back to Mia's heart.

He was glad that she was alert now, aware of her surroundings, and of those she was with. She needed to be awake to see with her own eyes what was being done.

When Mia looked quickly over at him, he smiled and nodded.

His smile seemed to reassure her. She returned it and relaxed even more.

She now gazed up at Talking Bird, patiently awaiting whatever he was going to do.

Her eyes widened when he opened the pouch and took out some of the tobacco, then laid the pouch aside and held the tobacco above the fire.

Instead of smoking the tobacco, he held it aloft, and looked directly into Mia's eyes.

"I will heal you, white woman, but you must also help yourself," Talking Bird said slowly. "You are stronger than you think. The spirits know this, and you must believe it, too. As I make the offering of tobacco, remember what I have said. Believe it."

Mia wasn't sure what she should do . . . nod . . . or just wait and see what came next.

She chose to give the old Shaman a nod and a smile, then watched and listened.

She was quite taken by the gentleness of his voice and by his efforts on her behalf.

"Ha-ho," Talking Bird said as he scattered the tobacco over the fire. "Fire, accept this offering of tobacco. Long ago, when I first learned of the magic that was given to me to use, you promised me aid if I offered you tobacco. Now I make that offering. I need your help to save this woman. Without your aid, she will die. This tobacco is my gift to you, and I pray that in return you will give her the gift of full health."

He took up more tobacco in his hand and again scattered it into the flames, but this time there was a response. The flames sputtered and sent sparks flying heavenward.

He smiled, for he knew that he had been heard. The purifying smoke had driven away the evil spirits that had caused the white woman to become ill. And this was good, for he had not been certain that the spirits that guided his people's lives would do the same for this woman, because she was a stranger and her skin was white.

Mia scarcely breathed as she watched what the Shaman would do next. He took several wooden vials from the many that he had placed on the floor around the base of his tepee.

She watched him take a wooden bowl and pour different liquids from the vials into it. Then he came to her and sat down beside her.

"I will now apply an herbal poultice to your

legs to relieve your discomfort," Talking Bird said, not hesitating to smooth the liquid over her rash. Mia gasped that he showed no fear of getting the terrible poison ivy himself.

"You can't," she suddenly said, scooting away from him. "You don't want this on your body. Please . . ."

"I do not fear such things," Talking Bird said, spreading the medicine across her legs. "I am protected by the spirits." He gazed over his shoulder at Wolf Hawk. "As is my grandson."

Mia glanced quickly past Talking Bird, at Wolf Hawk. Talking Bird's statement reminded her about seeing Wolf Hawk step from that mysterious mist, appearing from nowhere.

She could not help thinking that there were mysterious things happening that she might never understand. But no matter what she might suspect, it did not alter her feelings for Wolf Hawk.

In fact, as each moment passed, she cared more and more for him. It was not just gratitude. She was in love with him.

She had been so lost in thought, she hadn't realized that Talking Bird had finished putting the medicine on her legs, and had left her side for a moment. He returned carrying a wooden bowl.

She gazed questioningly at the bowl.

"I have brought you a bowl of Saskatoon berry broth to drink," he said. He held it aloft in the smoke over the fire, then offered it to her. "Drink. This, too, will make your body heal."

Unsure of drinking something that she had never heard of before, Mia didn't accept it.

Seeing her hesitance, Wolf Hawk went and leaned over to help Mia up to a sitting position.

"You must drink what is being offered you," Wolf Hawk softly encouraged. He took the bowl from his grandfather and placed it up close to Mia's lips. "Open your mouth. I shall help you."

"I . . . don't . . . know," Mia said, still hesitating.

Having unfamiliar medicine put on the outside of her body was one thing. But drinking it was something else. She was afraid of what she did not understand.

"You have put your trust in both myself and my grandfather. Why do you hesitate to drink something that will help your healing?" Wolf Hawk asked.

He gazed directly into her eyes.

He was glad when he saw trust returning to them, and was even happier when she smiled.

She turned to look into Talking Bird's eyes. "I'm sorry," she murmured. "I did not mean to look as though I don't trust you. Of course, I will drink your medicine."

She took the bowl from Wolf Hawk, and even though she was still afraid of it, she drank it, glad at least that it had a sweet, pleasant taste.

When she was finished, she handed the bowl back to Talking Bird. "Thank you," she murmured. "Thank you for everything."

"It is good of you to trust again," Talking Bird said, then placed a gentle hand on her shoulder and urged her again to a prone position. "Now you must sleep. Sleep brings with it cures, too. Rest and sleep are all important to those who are ill."

"I do feel so sleepy," Mia said, wondering now if the drink had something in it that would make her sleep. She glanced quickly up at Wolf Hawk. "I . . . trust . . . you both."

"I know," he said, wanting to take her into his arms and hold her. "And your trust is good. It will be rewarded. You will be healed. Sleep now, my woman. Sleep. I do assure you that you will be well again and very soon. My grandfather has made it so."

Unable to stay awake any longer, Mia fell into a restful sleep, no longer bothered by the hurtful itching, or fever.

Wolf Hawk and Talking Bird exchanged easy smiles.

"Take her to your own lodge now," Talking Bird said softly. "I have done all that is required for her. The rest is up to you."

"I understand," Wolf Hawk said, nodding.

He gazed at Mia with much love, then slowly lifted her into his arms.

He and his grandfather smiled at each other again; then Wolf Hawk carried Mia outside the tepee.

Knowing that Mia would not awaken anytime soon, Wolf Hawk changed into a mighty hawk, then gently grasped Mia in his powerful talons, and took flight.

He flew up past the wolf willows, through the

low-hanging fog, and soared across the river, until he came to a place in the forest where he could land without anyone seeing him.

After placing Mia on the ground, Wolf Hawk regained his human form, then again lifted Mia and ran with her toward his village.

When he entered, he took her quickly to his home, and soon had her resting comfortably on rich pelts close to the fire. He seated himself nearby so he could watch her.

"Soon you will be laughing and happy again," he whispered. He reached to her brow and softly brushed her hair back from it. "Soon I shall be able to touch you all over, not only your face. And you will want my touch. You will want more than touches from Wolf Hawk. I know you will, for you love me as I love you."

Mia seemed to hear his voice from somewhere far away.

She smiled at his words, for she now knew that he did love her. She now felt free to show her love for him.

Strange how a short while ago she seemed to be high in the air, floating and free, as though something were carrying her across the river.

She knew that with fever came hallucinations. Perhaps the drink she had been given had made the hallucinations even more pronounced.

No matter, though. She sensed that she was safe now. All would be well.

She knew it now without a doubt, and she could hardly wait to tell Wolf Hawk, for he was the one who had taken her to his grandfather to be healed. Again she drifted into a peaceful sleep.

She smiled as she slept, and Wolf Hawk saw and wondered what was causing such sweet dreams. He hoped it was he she was dreaming about.

Chapter Nineteen

O dream how sweet, too, sweet,
Too bitter sweet,
Whose wakening should have
Been in Paradise!
                              —Christina Rossetti

The fire in the fire pit had burned down to glowing embers. Today it would be allowed to burn itself out because the warm air outside the tepee made it unnecessary.

Mia lay on soft furs in Wolf Hawk's lodge, feeling quite comfortable. She was amazed at her progress. This morning she had discovered that her fever had broken and her legs were no longer swollen.

The poison ivy was no longer seeping, and even the sores seemed to be vanishing right before her eyes.

"My grandfather's medicine works," Wolf Hawk said as he entered his lodge and saw the surprise in Mia's eyes as she looked up at him.

"I cannot believe how quickly I am healing," Mia said, sitting up. She was so relieved that she felt better.

She was also glad to be away from Shadow Island. Although the Shaman had seemed to work miracles on her, the mysteriousness of the island had made her feel uneasy.

She had been surprised that Wolf Hawk had brought her to his own tepee to recuperate, instead of taking her to the one that had been assigned her. She could feel their connection strengthening and could no longer deny the feelings that overwhelmed her when she was with him. She had actually fallen in love with Wolf Hawk.

Even now, as he came over to her and knelt beside her, she could hardly control the rapid beating of her heart from just being so near him. Again she was keenly aware of the earthy, clean smell of him.

She loved the way his long, thick, black hair hung past his waist. She wanted to reach out and run her hands through it, but knew such boldness was not proper.

These feelings were new to her as a woman. She had doubted she would ever find a man she could love enough to want to marry.

Even though Wolf Hawk was an Indian and she was white, and she knew any relationship between them was forbidden, it did not matter at all to her.

She smiled at Wolf Hawk. "I do feel so much better," she murmured. She gestured with a hand toward her legs. "And look! My legs are no longer swollen and I am almost totally over the poison ivy."

She gazed up into his eyes. "How can I ever thank you enough for all that you have done for me, and . . . also your grandfather Shaman?" she said, smiling. "Had I not trusted you . . ."

"But you did, and you trusted my grandfather," Wolf Hawk said softly, smiling himself. "I know that at first you were wary of my grandfather's medicine, but it is good you trusted enough to allow him to care for you in the only way that he knows. I realize it is like nothing you've experienced before."

"No doctor that I ever knew could do what Talking Bird did for me," Mia murmured. "I would still be very ill had I gone to a white man's physician. I might have even lost one or both legs. But now? Look at them! I don't even believe I will be left with scars such as I have had in the past when I clumsily came into contact with poison ivy."

"My people's Great Spirit, which we call Earthmaker, looked down at you from his home in the sky. With his own wisdom he helped my grandfather heal you," Wolf Hawk said. He sat down beside her. "I noticed that you brought what is called a Bible with you when I asked you to choose some belongings to pack. I have heard that white people pray over that sort of talking leaves. Do you?"

"Talking leaves?" Mia murmured, lifting an eyebrow in curiosity. "What do you mean?"

"My people call all of your people's books 'talking leaves,'" Wolf Hawk said. "It is because they talk to you and teach you."

"That is an interesting way to describe books," Mia murmured. She smiled. "And, yes, to answer your question . . . I do pray as I read my Bible, and even when it is not with me. I prayed last night as I lay on my pallet of furs, with the moon looking down on me from the smoke hole. You see, when I pray, I am also communicating with my mama and papa, who are now in heaven."

She searched his eyes. "Do you and your people have something similar to a Bible that you use when you pray?" she asked softly.

"No, there is no written word for us to read as we worship and say our prayers," Wolf Hawk said, pleased that she would want to know about his people's beliefs. Surely that meant she cared for him.

"Then how do you pray, and when?" Mia asked.

She truly wanted to know. She wanted to learn everything about him, hoping that he, in turn, wished to know all about her. She wished he would openly confess his feelings about her.

She knew by his actions and behavior that he cared for her, but just how deeply? Would he ever let her know?

Or was it forbidden by his people's laws that a powerful Winnebago chief have feelings for a white woman?

And for herself, did she love this man enough to marry him?

Until she knew the answers to these questions, she knew that she must guard her words.

"There is so much to tell you about our beliefs, but I will explain a little each day," Wolf Hawk said.

"Please do," Mia murmured. "I am truly interested."

"The chief god we believe in is Earthmaker," he began. "He is sometimes known to my people as *Waxopini-zederea*, the Great Spirit. We pray to the Earthmaker, and from him we receive many blessings."

He paused, truly in awe of how interested she was in what he was saying. She gazed intensely at him while he spoke.

That was good, for he wanted to eventually teach her everything Winnebago.

"The women of the village also pray to the moon—" he began. He stopped abruptly when he saw Mia glance at the opened entrance flap, and heard her gasp.

"What is it?" he asked. He followed her gaze and saw nothing.

"Georgina," Mia softly cried.

Her pulse raced as she listened intently to the sounds outside the tepee.

She looked quickly at Wolf Hawk and reached out to grab his arm. "Do you hear it, too?" she cried. "Or is it my imagination?"

"Do I hear what?" Wolf Hawk asked, his eyes widening as the beautiful song of a bird unfamiliar to him came wafting into the lodge.

"Oh, my Lord, Wolf Hawk, it is," Mia said. She struggled to get to her feet, but fell back down on the pelts from weakness. "It . . . it . . . is my canary! It's Georgina! How could it be? How can she have survived the days and nights since Tiny loosed her from her cage?"

She clutched Wolf Hawk's arm more tightly.

"Please help me find her," Mia cried. "I can't let her fly away or I may never again get the chance to save her. Surely she can't survive much longer. She has never had to forage for her own food. And how has she eluded the night animals and the larger birds so long?"

Seeing her desperation, he gathered her up into his arms. As she clung to his neck with an arm, he quickly carried her outside.

Mia's heart skipped several beats, for now that she was outside, she no longer heard Georgina's song. Her bird had stopped singing.

She was filled with sudden panic, fearing that the canary had flown away. If so, she doubted she would ever find her again.

"She's gone," Mia said, suddenly sobbing. "As we stepped from your tepee the sudden movement must have frightened her away." She lowered her eyes in quiet despair. "I will never have her with me again. Never."

Suddenly a streak of yellow flashed before Mia's eyes. To her amazement, Georgina swept downward from somewhere in the trees and suddenly landed on Mia's arm.

When Mia saw Georgina's bold black eyes gaze up into hers, she felt that it was a miracle, for she had never attempted to train the canary to come to her.

"Georgina," Mia cried softly, as Wolf Hawk stood there, stunned at what had happened.

She looked quickly up at him. "This is my canary!" she said. "The bird I told you about. It's a miracle, Wolf Hawk. Look. She is sitting right on my arm. She is looking at me with such trust!"

"My woman, it is said among my people that if a bird comes to the door and gives its life up there, someone will die, but if it comes to the door and lives, it is a good omen . . . someone who is ill will live. Mia, your bird's appearance here proves that you will soon be completely well. I believe Shaman grandfather willed your bird here, as a blessing to you."

"Truly?" Mia said, her eyes wide as she gazed into Wolf Hawk's. "But how did he even know about her?"

"My grandfather knows all," Wolf Hawk said, smiling. "Even about this bird you call a canary."

"Your grandfather is a wonderful, blessed man," Mia murmured. "It is such a miracle that Georgina is with me again."

"Just as it is a miracle that you have appeared in my life when I needed a woman to be there," Wolf Hawk said, causing Mia a sensual thrill.

He knew this was not the time to go further into how he felt about Mia. At any moment the bird might fly away again.

If so, his woman would be terribly distressed and he could not allow that. He wanted everything good for her.

"Let us go inside my lodge with your bird," Wolf Hawk suggested, already carrying Mia through the entranceway.

He gently set her down on her feet, stunned when the bird still remained on her arm. At that moment it began warbling a beautiful, soft, sweet song.

"Do you hear her?" Mia whispered, just loud enough for Wolf Hawk to hear.

Then she thought of something else. She glanced up at Wolf Hawk.

"Her cage," she said. "I need her cage. She will feel at home only when she is in her familiar surroundings."

"I will go for her cage," Wolf Hawk said, already walking toward the entranceway. "I will return soon with it."

"Also her food," Mia said, stopping him. "There is a small package of bird food that I had left close to the cage. You will notice it when you get there. Please bring it to me, too."

Wolf Hawk nodded and started to leave again, but again her voice stopped him. "Thank you," Mia murmured. "Oh, Wolf Hawk, thank you."

"You rest while I am gone," he said. He gazed at the bird. "And I shall close the entrance flap so that your bird cannot fly away."

"I doubt that she will ever want to leave my side again," Mia said, laughing softly as Georgina continued to sing and gaze trustingly into Mia's eyes.

Nevertheless, Wolf Hawk closed the flap as he left. Minutes later he was on his horse, riding from the village.

Mia sat down on the pallet of furs with Georgina resting on the palm of her right hand. "You do not know what you have done for me by coming back today, my sweet bird," she murmured. "I am at peace, truly at peace, for the first time since my father's death. Now I feel as though I can allow myself to truly open up to my feelings for Wolf Hawk."

She stretched out on the pelts while Georgina rested quietly beside her.

As Georgina closed her eyes, and soon fell asleep, Mia wondered just how much rest her canary had managed to get while out there all alone in the world where danger lurked everywhere for such a tiny creature.

"I am safe . . . you are safe . . ." Mia whispered, tears of pure happiness shining in her eyes.

Chapter Twenty

Light, so low in the vale,
You flash and lighten afar,
For this is the golden morning
Of love!

—Alfred, Lord Tennyson

Wolf Hawk rode on his black steed with his chin held high and with a smile at the knowledge that Mia was going to be alright.

And it was a glorious thing to see her with the tiny yellow bird. She was so gentle with it, so loving.

He had always known, deep down, that she had a caring, gentle heart, but seeing her treat one of Earthmaker's tiny creatures with such love made him realize that she was exactly the sort of person he had always looked for in a wife.

The fact that her skin was white made no difference to him. It was her heart, her sweetness, that drew him to her.

The thought that he still had to convince his people of her goodness made his smile waver somewhat.

Whites had taken so much from the Winnebago, many had fallen into despair as they had been forced off their land, to be penned up like animals on reservations.

Wolf Hawk felt so fortunate that under his leadership the Bird Clan had avoided such treatment. He had made sure that they found a place far from the interference of whites.

The sign that whites had ever been in the area was the old fort, and that had been abandoned long before Wolf Hawk had led his people to the Rush River, where they built their homes and planted their crops.

He would meet in council soon with his warriors and explain to them what he planned to do . . . request Mia's hand in marriage.

He would explain that she was a woman alone in the world, that she had no kin who would come for her and cause trouble to his Bird Clan. He would explain that were he to send her from their village, she would have nowhere to go, and no one to go to. She would be left to wander, to drift, and possibly to die at the hand of someone evil who might rape, then kill her.

No. He would not allow that to happen. He would make his warriors, his people as a whole, understand Mia's plight.

In time, his people would all know and understand. But if it took them longer than it should, he would go ahead and do as his heart was leading him to do.

He was chief. What he said was final, always, at their village.

Suddenly his thoughts were stilled when he saw

something on the ground that made him draw rein. He dismounted and knelt down, plucking from the ground a card such as he knew was used by gamblers.

He had seen them at a trading post and he had asked about them. The white man in charge of the post had explained to him what the cards were used for. He had been told that men sometimes killed one another over those cards.

A breeze brought another card to Wolf Hawk's feet, and then another and another. He looked beyond them and saw others scattered across the land, colorful against the dullness of the ground.

He went and gathered them up, then stopped and studied them as they lay in his hand. He recalled Mia talking about the man whose name fit his tiny stature, and how he loved to gamble. She had said he carried a deck of cards with him at all times.

"These could be his," he whispered to himself.

He stood and looked slowly around him, then searched the ground again for footprints. He saw none other than those he and his horse had made.

He gathered from the lack of footprints that these cards had blown here from somewhere else.

But where?

And why would the man who owned them allow them to leave his possession?

"Unless . . ." he whispered, again slowly looking all around him.

Yes, something might have happened to the man who owned the cards.

Then another thought came to him.

These cards didn't necessarily have to be Tiny's. They could have belonged to the two trappers who were fleeing the Winnebago's wrath.

If so, were the men still in the area? Were they hiding until they felt it was safe to come out of cover?

If those men were nearby, they could have a gun aimed at him this very moment.

He stiffened as he gathered the cards together in one pile, then stuffed them inside the travel bag that hung at the side of his horse.

Before mounting his steed, he again looked cautiously in all directions, but he saw nothing. Nor did he hear anyone or anything except the soft breeze that whispered through the trees all around him.

He swung himself into his saddle, grabbed the reins, then rode onward, but this time not with the same easiness he had felt before he found the cards.

He could be the hunted one now.

He rode stiffly, his eyes ever watching around him for any sudden movement. And then he spotted something lying on the ground, and a flash of something red caught in an elm tree's bark. Again, he drew his steed to a halt.

"A shoe," he mumbled to himself as he gazed intently at the lone shoe that lay on the ground a few feet from his horse.

He then focused on what was stuck to the bark of the tree. His eyebrows lifted when he realized it was strands of hair that made a brilliant red streak against the grayish brown color of the trunk of the old elm tree.

He gazed at the shoe again, and then at the hair. He recalled the man named Tiny having that color hair, and the shoe was not of a large size.

Ho, yes, it did seem to all fit together. Had Tiny come to a bad end?

But how would he have died?

Was it an animal, perhaps a large bear, that had killed the tiny man? Or was it perhaps those two trappers who had murdered him?

If he were dead, where was his body?

No matter how it had happened, or where the body might be, if what he was thinking were true, Wolf Hawk knew that he, himself, could also be in danger.

He hurriedly dismounted, whisked the shoe up from the ground, adding it to the travel bag with the cards, then carefully plucked the hair from the tree and put it with Tiny's other belongings. Then he mounted and rode quickly through the forest until he finally reached the fort.

Feeling vulnerable, he didn't go on inside the walls of the fort until he'd studied the footprints going in and out of it.

He saw only one set of fresh prints. They went into the fort, and then the same prints came out again.

He dismounted, took the shoe that he had found from the travel bag, and set it directly onto the footprint; the shoe belonged to whoever had made those footprints.

"Tiny," he said, his jaw tight.

Ho, by the smallness of the print and the shoe, he judged that Tiny had returned to the fort after Wolf Hawk had taken Mia from it. Then he had left again.

Sighing, feeling safe enough now to enter the fort and get the bird's cage, Wolf Hawk placed the shoe back inside his travel bag and walked his horse through the wide gate to the cabin where Mia had stayed with her father and Tiny.

Securing his horse's reins, he stepped gingerly inside the cabin, finding it as deserted as he'd thought it would be.

He smiled when he saw the cage right where Mia had said it would be. Not wanting to take any more time than he needed to, he looked around and found what he thought was the seed that the bird ate.

He placed it inside the cage, then grabbed the cage and took it outside to his horse.

After tying it to the side of the saddle, he mounted and rode directly back to his village without stopping.

When he stepped inside his tepee, holding the cage before him, Mia looked quickly up.

Georgina was trustingly asleep on her lap. Smiling at Wolf Hawk, Mia reached a hand out for the cage as she whispered, "Thank you" to him.

Wolf Hawk returned the smile, then set the cage close beside her.

He knelt there and watched her gently place the bird in the cage. When Georgina saw that she was back inside her home, she leapt up to her main perch and began singing.

Mia sighed. "Isn't she such a beautiful thing?" she said, slowly closing the door. "Her song is so sweet. My bird is a miracle! How did she survive without her cage? Without me?"

"It is not for us to question," Wolf Hawk said, reaching over and gently touching Mia's cheek. "It is good to see how happy your bird makes you. I am glad that I have been able to add to that happiness by bringing her back home to you."

"I can never thank you enough," Mia murmured, reaching up and taking his hand from her face, then gently holding it. "You are so kind. Thank you, thank you."

The feel of her hand in his made Wolf Hawk again realize the depths of his love for this woman.

He knew then what he must do, and he would do it tomorrow. There was a special ritual that was performed by a Winnebago warrior when he was in love. And Wolf Hawk was ready to undertake it.

Tomorrow!

"May I ask something else of you?" Mia questioned, searching his eyes.

"Ask," Wolf Hawk said, looking intently back at her, their eyes locked. "Ask and it shall be done."

"Would you bring some fresh water for Georgina's water well, while I give her food?" Mia asked softly.

"I am happy to see you so happy," Wolf Hawk said, going to his store of water, which was kept in a long, buckskin bag hanging right inside his lodge.

He watched Mia place food in the bird's food well, and then take the water well from the cage and handed it to him.

"Fill it half full," Mia murmured. "That is enough for such a tiny thing."

When everything was done to make Georgina's comfort complete, Wolf Hawk took Mia's hands and held them as he gazed into her eyes again.

"I found something while I was on my way to the fort," he said soberly. "What I found is in my travel bag. I shall go and get it from my horse. I will show you what I found."

Mia was all eyes when he left and waited anxiously for him to return to the tepee.

When he did, she gasped softly at the sight of the many cards that he had found on the ground.

He placed them on the mat at their feet, and then reached inside his bag and retrieved the lone shoe . . . and the strands of hair, which he placed next to the cards.

"Lordie be," Mia murmured, paling at the sight of the hair and the shoe.

She studied them for only a moment, then gazed again into Wolf Hawk's eyes. "These things are Tiny's," she said. "I know the shoe. I . . . I . . . know the hair, and of course, I know whose cards these are. All of them are Tiny's."

"I thought so," Wolf Hawk said, nodding.

"Tiny would never leave his cards behind, for he

is a gambler," she said, swallowing hard. "Surely this means that he has come to a bad end."

She slowly shook her head back and forth. "I wonder if the trappers killed him?" she asked softly. "I wonder if they are still close by?"

Then she reached out and touched Wolf Hawk on the arm. "I never cared anything at all for Tiny," she murmured. "But . . . he might still be alive, and out there, helpless. Do you think that you could go and search for him? While you are doing that, you could also search for those two men again. Perhaps it wasn't they who stole the scow and fled in it. If they are still somewhere close by, hiding, you might be able to catch them."

"I can understand why you would want me to search for the murderers, but why would you care for that tiny man who caused you nothing but trouble?" he asked, taking her hand from his arm and holding it.

"I am a Christian, that's why," Mia said softly. "I have never truly wished this man harm. He is probably a victim of his upbringing. Perhaps he never had anyone to show him love. I just think it is the right thing to do to see if he is alive out there somewhere, afraid, perhaps hungry."

"You never cease to amaze me. You always seem to show kindness to others, even those who have wronged you," Wolf Hawk said thickly. "You are such a giving person."

"I behave how I was raised to behave," Mia murmured. "My papa and mama were very loving people. I . . . I . . . inherit this all from them."

"I will go now and gather up some warriors. We will search for the tiny man to see if he is still alive," Wolf Hawk said softly.

He released her hand reluctantly. He wanted to do much more than hold her hand. He wanted her in his embrace.

But now was not the time to let her know just how deeply he felt for her.

Tomorrow.

"Go with care, and . . . and . . . thank you," Mia said, following him to the entrance flap. She held it aside for him.

He turned and gazed into her eyes one more time before leaving.

Mia stood in the entranceway and watched Wolf Hawk go from tepee to tepee, seeking help from one warrior and then another.

A sudden thought made her heart turn cold. What if she were sending him to his death?

She started to rush out of the tepee and tell Wolf Hawk that she had changed her mind, but it was too late. He was already riding from the village with many of his men dutifully following him.

"What have I done?" she cried softly in despair, watching until she couldn't see him any longer.

Georgina began warbling a sweet song again.

Mia went to the cage and sat down beside it. "I'm afraid of what I have encouraged Wolf Hawk to do," she said. "So afraid."

Chapter Twenty-one

Come and let us live, my Deare,
Let us love and never feare!
　　　　—*Catullus* (Gaius Valerius Catullus)

Wolf Hawk had returned to his tepee with the news that he doubted Tiny was still alive. He and his warriors had searched far and wide but had seen no sign of him anywhere.

Mia had conflicting feelings about this news.

She had always despised the tiny man, then had actually hated him when she found out that he had released Georgina to the wild, but she had never wished him dead.

Now she, too, believed that Tiny was dead. She doubted that she would ever see him again.

She had wanted him to disappear from her life many times when she had been stuck with Tiny on the scow. The little man had aggravated not only herself, but also her father. But she would never wish for something this bad to happen to him . . . that he would just disappear from the face of the earth.

The breeze was cool on her face and arms as it wafted through the raised entrance flap of Wolf Hawk's tepee.

Her health had improved so much, she felt that

today might be the day she would be asked to return to the lodge that had been prepared for her prior to her illness.

"It's a miracle," she whispered to herself as she raised the hem of the beautiful doeskin dress that had been given to her by Wolf Hawk's cousin Little Snowbird.

The horrible sores made by the poison ivy were all but gone.

Only a few of the largest were still visible, but they would soon disappear, too.

She ran her hands slowly over the smoothness of one of her legs. She was amazed at how fast she had gotten well.

Talking Bird had truly worked magic on her.

She wondered how an Indian Shaman could know so much more about medicine than the doctors in the white community? When she had had poison ivy before, it had taken many weeks for Dr. Jamieson's cure to heal her.

Perhaps Talking Bird had more faith in his abilities than the white doctors had in theirs. Or . . . perhaps it was pure magic!

In any case, she was well now. Should she wish to, she was strong enough to go on her way.

More than once Wolf Hawk had said that she was free to go whenever she wished, yet at the same time he'd told her he hoped that she would choose to stay.

He had not gone so far as to ask her to be his wife, yet she knew that was in his heart. She could tell by the way he looked at her, with gazes that melted her heart.

She ached to be in his arms, to be held by him. Her lips quivered even now with want of his kiss.

"What am I doing?" she said aloud, causing Georgina to hop from one perch to another at the sound of Mia's voice.

Her canary began singing, the sound so sweet it made Mia again thank God above that her bird had been saved from harm in the forest. It gave her shivers to think of what could have happened, but she refused to dwell on painful thoughts of the past.

She had a decision to make. She must decide what her future held for her.

She did have her parents' home waiting for her in St. Louis, but that was all. There were no relatives in the city. Mia would be alone.

She had cousins, aunts and uncles scattered across the country. But it took money to travel and she had nothing.

If she had had the scow, she could have sold it for enough money to help her fend for herself for awhile. And, of course, she could sell her St. Louis home.

But somehow that plan did not seem appealing. Her family had never been close. In fact, she could count on the fingers of one hand how often her parents had invited their family members to their home.

So she doubted that any of them would relish

the idea of Mia coming to live with them. She would be only an intrusion on their lives.

"Mama, Papa," she whispered, gazing up through the smoke hole toward the blue sky. "What should I do?"

She was feeling more comfortable with the death of her parents now. Wolf Hawk had told her that after a person loses someone they love, they must carry on with life, for death was a natural thing.

He had told her that losing a loved one was difficult, yet one should be happy for the departed, for they were now without pain or sadness. They were with their ancestors in the sky, happy to see them again.

That should be celebrated, not regretted.

It was hard, but she knew that she must not succumb to the emptiness in her heart caused by her parents' deaths.

Her deep thoughts were interrupted by the sound of whispering from somewhere behind her. She looked quickly around and her eyes widened when she saw several children standing just outside the entranceway to the tepee.

They were whispering to one another as they watched and listened to Georgina. The canary was still singing, and its song had reached outside to the children who were at play.

Mia smiled and reached a hand out toward them. She beckoned for them to come inside.

"Come and see my bird up close if you wish," Mia offered. "She loves an audience."

The children didn't have to be asked a second time. They almost fell over one another as they scrambled inside, then sat in a circle around the cage.

Georgina didn't seem at all perturbed by this sudden audience. In fact she hopped back and forth on her perch as she continued sweetly singing.

Mia stood away from the children, watching and smiling. She had always loved children but had never had the chance to be around many.

Even as a child, she had led a mostly solitary life. Her mother had taught her everything that other children learned in a school house.

She had felt a certain emptiness inside that came with not being able to associate with other children. But that, too, had passed, for she had accepted the life her parents had made for her. She had loved them too much to cause problems over anything that they had chosen for her.

Mia covered a soft laugh behind a hand when she looked at Georgina and saw how the bird seemed to be strutting as she moved along the perch. It seemed as though Georgina had missed having an audience, for she seemed to be singing her heart out, to entertain . . . to please.

Suddenly Mia felt another presence in the tepee. She turned and felt the heat of a blush rush to her cheeks when she found Wolf Hawk standing behind her.

He had apparently heard Georgina singing and had seen the children enter his lodge. He had came to join the happy group inside.

He saw the warmth in Mia's eyes as she smiled and stepped back to stand beside him.

"Isn't it sweet?" she asked, gazing into Wolf Hawk's dark, beautiful eyes. "The bird loves the children as much as they love her."

"They not only enjoy your bird's song, but are also amazed to see a bird in a cage that is happy to be there," Wolf Hawk said.

He took her hand and led her farther away from the children so that he could talk to Mia without disturbing them.

"Even I find that very unusual," he said. "Yet I can tell the bird is happy. If it were not content, it would not sing such a beautiful song."

"My canary has a reason to sing because she knows that she is safe inside the cage and will be fed and watered."

She frowned a little as she glanced over at Georgina. "But I wonder what I shall feed her when my supply of birdseed runs out," she said softly.

Then she gazed into Wolf Hawk's eyes again. She smiled. "I know what I shall do," she murmured. "I shall go to Talking Bird and ask him what I can feed my bird so that she will stay healthy and content."

Wolf Hawk's heart skipped a beat, for he felt that Mia's words indicated she wasn't ready to leave the village. There seemed enough food in the bag to last for a long while, for the bird ate only small amounts at a time.

It made his heart swell to believe that Mia did want to stay with his people, and with him.

Ah, but he felt so deeply for her! He was eager to let her know just how much.

Tomorrow. She would know tomorrow.

Chapter Twenty-two

I would ask of you, my darling,
A question soft and low,
That gives me many a heartache,
As the moments come and go.

—*Anonymous*

At first light, Wolf Hawk had awakened and left his lodge while Mia still slept.

Wearing only a breechcloth, moccasins and his knife sheathed at his right side, his hair held back with a headband that he had quickly slid into place as he walked from his tepee, he now made his way through the forest.

His eyes were ever searching for two plants that he was going to use for his courting medicine.

He smiled as he thought of Mia sleeping so soundly and trustingly inside his lodge. He had to make certain that she wouldn't be aware of what he was doing when he knelt at her side with the medicine.

His Shaman grandfather had taught him which plants should be used once he found a woman he favored more than any other, one he trusted would be faithful to him until they were both gray and could only sit and smile at each other while others did the work they had once done.

Ah, but those years were still far ahead of them. First, they would share a lifetime of love and happiness.

He could already envision the children born of their love.

The girls would be heartbreakingly pretty, with their mother's eyes and their father's hair. Their skin color mattered not at all, for they would be the children of a proud Winnebago chief and his wondrous wife.

The sons would have all the traits required to be great warriors, and one of them would step into the moccasins of his father as chief of the Bird Clan of Winnebago.

It was good to think of these things as Wolf Hawk continued to travel light-footed in his moccasins over the various flowering plants that reached out beyond the forest, where sunshine washed them with its warmth and light through the day, bringing the smiling faces of the flowers fully abloom.

Wolf Hawk slowed his steps, looking more carefully for the two flowers he sought.

He carried a small pouch, in which he would place the flowers. Then he would carry them back to his lodge to prepare the magic potion with which he would anoint his true love. When she awakened from her night's slumber and saw him sitting beside her, he would know without a doubt that she would favor him as her husband.

He was anxious to see her awaken, to witness the look on her face when she realized that things had changed between them, even though she would not know why, or how. She would just know how much he desired her. And the potion would ensure that she desired him just as much.

Then a few days later they would have the marriage ceremony that would make them husband and wife in the eyes of his people.

He knew that Mia would be thinking of her parents that day and wishing they could share these happy moments with her and Wolf Hawk, for women felt deeply about these things. He would reassure her that they were there, in spirit, holding hands, happy on this day that guaranteed their daughter would be loved and safe forevermore.

As he continued searching, he thought about the courting medicine. It was made of a plant that could be recognized by its blue flowers. The Winnebago believed that there was a male plant and a female plant.

He knew that when he found the plants, he could not dig them unless he found them growing side by side, with the male growing to the east of the female. For this reason it was very hard to find the flowers.

As he continued to walk he heard a cardinal crooning loudly from the treetops. Hearing the bird reminded Wolf Hawk of Mia's canary, whose song was as sweet as the cardinal's.

Then suddenly his eyes widened. It was as though the beautiful cardinal had led him to the plants that he had been searching for.

Right there, at his feet, were the two flowers in question.

He gazed up at the cardinal, which still sat in the tree a few feet away, and said a grateful "thank-you" to him. Then he knelt and studied the two plants more carefully.

He looked skyward to judge the position of the sun. He was glad to see the two plants grew the way they should in order for him to be able to use them and know the magic would work for him. They grew close together and the male plant was at the female's east side.

He smiled when he knew that all conditions had been fulfilled. He took his knife from its sheath.

Carefully, even prayerfully, he dug both plants from the ground, then laid the knife aside and tangled the roots of the plants together.

After that was done he pinched the blue flower from its stem and plucked off the center leaf of the female plant. Then he placed the flower, the leaf and the roots in the pouch tied to his breechclout's waistband.

He held the small pouch in his hand and gazed heavenward and said a quiet *wa-do*, thank-you, to the Earthmaker, then tied the pouch to his waistband again and headed for home.

When he arrived at his village, no one was yet stirring from their beds. All was quiet except for the soft melodies of birds in the nearby forest.

Then a thought came to Wolf Hawk that made him stop almost in midstep.

The canary in his lodge. What if the bird was awakened by Wolf Hawk's entrance into his tepee? Georgina might awaken Mia.

That would not give Wolf Hawk time enough to grind the plants together before placing the mixture on Mia's body.

Then he recalled something else.

Mia had told him the bird would sleep until she lifted the cover from the cage.

Relieved, Wolf Hawk continued on inside his tepee.

He stopped and smiled down at the sleeping woman who would soon be his in every way.

She looked as lovely in her sleep as she did when she was awake. Yet he preferred her awake, for he loved to look into her eyes. They were mystically beautiful and seemed always to speak to him even when Mia was saying nothing aloud.

It was the sort of communication that was possible between two people in love, as he and Mia were!

He gazed over at the covered cage. He heard no sound from it.

Wolf Hawk stepped lightly past the cage to the back of the tepee and lifted a small earthen pot from many others.

He set it on the floor of his lodge. He removed the flower, leaf and roots from his small pouch, then dropped them all into the pot.

Taking a small rock, he quietly ground all of these together thoroughly, until a paste was all that lay at the bottom of the jar.

He put the rock aside, gazed at Mia again, then lifted the pot in one hand and tiptoed over to where she lay.

He watched her eyes for a moment, to make sure she was not awakening. When he saw that she was still very much asleep, he reached his fingers inside the jar and gathered some of the crushed remains between two fingers.

Then, ever so lightly, he touched several places on Mia's body that were not covered by the gown she wore. Softly he slid a hand inside the gown and gently rubbed some of the mixture on the silken skin just above her heart.

She sighed in her sleep, but her eyes remained closed. Oh, how he was tempted to touch the fullness of her breast, but he knew he must keep his desires reined in for now. Carefully, he withdrew his hand from beneath the gown.

He sprinkled some of the mixture on the top of her head, and some beneath her nose so that she would smell it upon awakening. Then he put everything away so that once she was awake she would not see the pot or question him about its contents.

Smiling, oh, so loving her, Wolf Hawk went back to her and knelt at her side.

He bent low and brushed a soft kiss across her lips. He could smell the scent of the mixture that he had placed just beneath her nose.

Mia awakened with a start, then smiled when she saw Wolf Hawk sitting beside her.

"I had a strange dream," she murmured as she

leaned up on an elbow. She scratched idly at the skin just above her lips. "But now I cannot remember what it was, or even what it was about."

She blushed as she lowered her lashes, then gazed at Wolf Hawk again. "Did you awaken me with a kiss or was I also dreaming that?" she asked, searching his eyes.

"The kiss was real," Wolf Hawk said, then reached for her and drew her up against his warm body. "Do you wish for another?"

Mia nodded, then melted inside when his lips came down on hers in an all-consuming kiss.

She clung to him and crawled onto his lap, oh, so ready for whatever he wished to do to her this morning.

It seemed magical, somehow, that he was there with her today, his kisses awakening everything sensual within her. She knew that were he to ask, she would even surrender her virginity to him.

She ached strangely for him.

She felt as though she couldn't go any longer without knowing the true joy of making love with this man . . . the man she would forever adore.

"I need you," Wolf Hawk whispered against her lips, so happy that the magic potion had worked.

Chapter Twenty-three

Let wish and magic
Work at will in you.

—*Driscoll*

Seeing things in visions that no one else could see, Talking Bird always paid heed to his dreams. The night before he'd dreamt of two men approaching the land of the Winnebago. Talking Bird knew them to be the trappers who were responsible for the two young braves' deaths.

Deep down inside himself he had known these men would return. How could they not? They had left many valuable furs behind.

Talking Bird smiled at his grandson's cleverness in commanding his warriors to take the pelts from their hiding place and bring them to their village.

He knew that the men had many miles yet to travel on the Rush River before arriving back at the fort, where they thought their pelts were still hidden. Talking Bird had plenty of time to pray to the Earthmaker. He had his own way of dealing with whites who foolishly came on the land of the Winnebago.

The white-skinned woman with whom his grandson was infatuated was different. Although Talking Bird would have rathered his grandson took a Winnebago woman as his wife, it was not Talking Bird's place to interfere or tell his chieftain grandson his opinion about such things.

Wolf Hawk was a grown man, a great leader, and a man of much intelligence. If his heart told him that he loved a woman with white skin, so be it.

But Talking Bird would not allow anyone else with white skin to interfere in his people's lives. The woman was an exception. She was all alone in the world. No one would come to his people's village to search for her.

She was now Wolf Hawk's woman, no one else's, and Talking Bird would give his grandson his blessings, soon.

The sun spiraled down through the smokehole onto Talking Bird as he prepared to pray.

Today his thick white hair was worn in a long, lone braid down his back. The tunic had designs of nature embroidered on it, which had been sewn there by several women of his village who were skilled at beadwork.

His moccasins were also beaded, as was the medicine bundle in which he kept his sacred pipe.

The beads were of beautiful colors. Red like the cardinals that flitted through the air, blue like the sky over Shadow Island, and green like the cool, soft grass upon which he walked.

Talking Bird had many supernatural powers. He could will the river to part with only one blink of his old eyes or cause the ground to quake and shake, leaving large cracks in Mother Earth.

Planning to use his powers today, he lifted his

buckskin medicine bundle onto his lap. The fire's glow shadowed his ancient face.

His long, lean fingers slowly opened the bundle. He reached inside. He took from it his sacred calumet pipe. He gently laid the pipe beside him, then again reached inside his medicine bundle and withdrew a smaller bag from it, which held the sacred tobacco.

He opened this bag, then lifted the pipe from the thick fur of the bear, and shook tobacco into the bowl until there was enough to smoke and pray to the Earthmaker. It would not be on trappers alone that he would cast a spell. He would also invoke the waters that cradled the boat carrying them closer and closer to the fort.

He smiled at their foolishness in returning.

He took a small twig from the lodge fire and held it to the tobacco in his pipe.

He puffed long and hard until he felt the tobacco smoke deep inside his lungs and knew the pipe was going well enough to be used for his prayers.

He took the pipe from his mouth. He held it heavenward and gazed up. He looked through the smoke hole and began speaking his feelings to the Earthmaker.

"Earthmaker, to whom my words are spoken today, I hold this pipe up to you," he said softly. His old eyes watched the smoke spiral slowly through the smoke hole.

He again placed the pipe in his mouth, puffing hard on it, then exhaling so that the smoke wreathed around him.

Again, he took the pipe from his mouth. He turned it in all four directions, then held it down toward the earth. Once he had honored the spirits with whom he was communicating, he rested the bowl of the pipe on his knee. He could hear the spirits whispering all around him as he said, "There are two evil white men who have wronged our people, not only taking animals and furs on land that is usually hunted by the Winnebago, but also the lives of two of our beloved youths. I ask you to watch for these men as they grow closer and closer. It is my fervent desire that the river water shake with an earthquake of your doing, but not enough to harm my people who are on nearby land."

He bowed his head, then looked above again, through the smoke, and smiled, for he knew that what he had prayed for would be granted him.

He had never disappointed the spirits, nor had they him.

Chapter Twenty-four

Quick!
I want!
And who can tell what tomorrow may befall—
Love me more, or not at all.

—Sill

As Wolf Hawk held Mia ever so close in his arms, kissing her, she clung passionately to him. She had never known such feelings could exist and had not even fantasized about being with a man like this.

But it seemed natural to be there with Wolf Hawk, becoming oh, so dizzy, the longer his lips lingered on hers.

And then she drew quickly away from him, her eyes wide, as she gazed down at the mats on the floor of the tepee. She looked quickly up at him.

"Did you feel that?" she gasped out, searching his eyes. "Did you hear it? The floor trembled for a moment and I even heard a strange sort of rumbling, but now both are gone. Did you experience the same thing? It felt like the beginning of an earthquake, but thank goodness it stopped."

Wolf Hawk smiled at her. He reached out and took her by the hand, then led her to a thick pallet of furs. "Come and sit with me," he said, leading her down to sit beside him. "What you felt and heard happens sometimes, but rarely have my people experienced an earthquake serious enough to do harm to our village or our lives. There seems to be a weakness of the ground where we have made our home. Perhaps that is one reason white people do not make their homes here."

Wolf Hawk had not told her the full truth. He understood the magic of his grandfather and he felt that what had just occurred was his grandfather's doing.

Wolf Hawk was not alarmed. He knew that his grandfather only caused the earth to shake for good reason.

Wolf Hawk did not know why his grandfather had chosen to use his powers today, but he never questioned Talking Bird's power.

If his grandfather saw a need for an earthquake, so be it.

"But aren't you afraid that the earthquake might come in full force some day and kill you all?" Mia asked.

She looked toward the closed entrance flap, wondering if everyone beyond it had experienced the same tremors as she and Wolf Hawk.

She didn't hear any excitement or cries of terror outside, so if his people had felt and heard the shaking, they were no more excited than Wolf Hawk.

"Do you see fear in my eyes?" Wolf Hawk asked, smiling at Mia.

"No," she murmured.

"Then you should not be afraid, either," Wolf Hawk said softly. "I will not allow anything to harm you ever again."

He smiled into her eyes. "Our Earthmaker keeps us safe," he said, still holding her hand.

Before she had become alarmed, Wolf Hawk had felt the yearning in Mia's kiss and the way she had clung to him. She had even pressed her body against his as though to tell him that she accepted them as a true couple now.

That was what he desired from the bottom of his heart. He wanted her to want him as badly, as deeply, as he ached to have her. Not only for a moment or two, but forever.

He wanted to make her his wife.

"Your Earthmaker is something like my God, I am sure, yet God doesn't always stop bad things from happening," Mia murmured, seeing her father's grave in her mind's eye.

"Nor did your Earthmaker keep the two young braves who died in the traps safe," Mia went on.

She saw his body stiffen. He seemed affronted that she was questioning his people's god.

She lowered her eyes, then looked up into his again. "I'm sorry," she murmured. "I shouldn't have said that about your Earthmaker. I apologize."

"You never need apologize to me about anything," Wolf Hawk said. He placed a hand on her cheek, loving its softness. Her skin was as soft as were her lips against his.

"Just as in your world, your god cannot guard

your people against all evil, so it was with the trappers who caused the deaths of our young braves," he said. "It is just the way of life . . . birth, death, and . . . happiness. I have learned that one must take from life what is given, both bad and good. But it is true that the Earthmaker is always there for my people in all ways when his guidance is needed. I'm sure you pray to your god for the same sort of guidance."

"I understand that sometimes misfortunes occur, such as my stepping into those poison ivy vines before I realized it," Mia murmured. "I understand that neither God, nor your Earthmaker, can reach down suddenly from the sky and keep those types of things from happening. I also realize that life is ruled by both good and evil, and that everyone must do what they can in order to have good on their side."

She smiled at him, loving the way he rested his hand on her cheek. The touch of his flesh against hers made it hard for her to think.

She ached for his kiss again, for the feel of his body against hers.

These things were new to her.

These feelings!

These wants!

These yearnings!

"I know that you have told me I don't need to thank you for things you have done for me, but I must thank you again for what you did for me when I was so ill," she said.

She was unable to keep herself from shuddering with the memory of how awful she had felt. She stretched her legs out before her and ran a hand down the smoothness of one of them. "It's a miracle that my skin is not left scarred," she murmured. "The sores were so horrible."

She turned to him, and as his hand fell away from her cheek, she held it between hers. "I shall always be grateful for what you have done for me," she said, her voice breaking. "You took me in your own home and cared for me even though I was no more than a stranger to you, a woman you first saw as your enemy."

She fell into his embrace as he wrapped her gently in his arms and held her close.

He laid her down on the plush pelts, then moved atop her so that his body gently pressed against hers. She moaned with ecstasy when his lips came to her mouth in a passionate kiss.

She felt as though she were melting inside as she returned the kiss and twined her arms around his neck. She couldn't believe that she'd ever thought him guilty of evil things. She knew now that he could not possibly be responsible for the death of her mother. She knew that he was not guilty of her father's death. It was her father's weak heart that had taken him from Mia.

No, it was truly not Wolf Hawk's fault that Mia had been left without a mother and father. He was kind and generous and loving, everything Mia's father had been.

She had always said that she wanted to marry a man just like her father, who had been so gentle with his wife and daughter in every way.

Mia was becoming almost mindless with desire as the kiss deepened and Wolf Hawk began kneading one of her breasts through the soft doeskin of her dress. The mere touch of his hand there made her feel as though she might faint from the desire that was sweeping through her.

And when his other hand reached down and began moving slowly up the inside of one of her legs, touching places that seemed to come alive beneath his exploring fingers, Mia sucked in a wild breath of desire.

When his fingers touched that place where her heart seemed suddenly centered, where no man's hands had been before, she could feel something wonderful being aroused in her. It was a sweetness, a spiraling pleasure, that she never knew existed.

He caressed her where she now throbbed with a need she had never known before. She clutched his neck as he twined his fingers through the strands of auburn hair at the juncture of her thighs, then sank one of those fingers slowly into her. She knew she should not allow such intimacies until she was a married woman, but she just couldn't stop him. She had never felt anything so deliciously wonderful as the feelings being awakened inside her.

It was as though something was ready to explode with ecstasy throughout her.

"I can stop if you wish me to," Wolf Hawk suddenly whispered into her ear, yet he did not miss one stroke inside her with his finger.

He knew he was arousing her for the first time in her life, for her innocence was plain to see. She was not the sort to let just any man touch and caress her.

He could hardly consider stopping what he had initiated, for his loins were on fire with need, his manhood tight and throbbingly hot.

But he knew the kind of woman she was and did not want to cause her to feel shame if they did continue.

Almost too mindless to think, Mia was breathless with the pleasure that was overwhelming her. Oh, how could she ask him to stop when everything within her cried out to be with him totally, to share with him what she knew they both wanted?

Of course she knew what her mother had taught her about sinning with a man before vows were spoken.

But since so much had happened to her, and she had realized just how quickly one's world could be changed, she had a new attitude toward life and love. Who was to say there would even be another tomorrow for her or Wolf Hawk?

"I will marry you soon," Wolf Hawk said softly as he leaned away from her and gazed into her wondering eyes. "Yet if you would rather wait to make love until vows are spoken between us, I will understand."

Seeing that he did respect her and was actually willing to wait, Mia felt her eyes mist with grateful tears. She had known that he was not the sort to force anything on a woman.

She had instigated their lovemaking as much as he, for something inside her cried out for his caresses and kisses.

Even the fact that she had allowed him access to that place where only she had touched, as she had washed herself so delicately, proved to her just how much she did trust and need him.

She placed a gentle hand on his cheek, her own hot with a blush. "I don't think I can wait after realizing just how much I need you," she murmured. "Wolf Hawk, I love you so dearly. And I do believe that you will marry me, so, my love, I do not think I can bear another moment without you making love to me. I . . . I . . . love you. Oh, how I do love you."

"I do not know how it happened, but I fell in love with you almost as soon as I met you. But I could not act out that love, for at that moment I was not certain what your being at the fort with your father and that tiny man truly meant," he said huskily.

He reached a hand up and gently smoothed several locks of fallen hair back from her flushed cheeks.

"Were you to have been associated with those trappers, you would have been my enemy forever," he said thickly.

"But neither I, my father, or Tiny had anything

to do with them," Mia said. "It was just coincidence that we happened to be where those evil men hid the pelts."

"*Ho*, I believe you, and I regret that I did not know the truth from the beginning, for I could have possibly helped your father by taking him to Talking Bird for his special medicine," Wolf Hawk said, now tenderly rubbing her cheek with a finger. "That was not meant to be. But you and I are."

He brushed a soft kiss across her lips. "We were meant to be," he repeated. "We were meant to meet and come together. When we wed, we will be as one until a child is born of our love. Then we will be three, not two."

"A child," Mia sighed. She adored the thought of having a baby, especially with Wolf Hawk fathering it. "A son? A daughter? I so badly wish to have both. I was raised as an only child. It was lonely, Wolf Hawk, ever so lonely."

"I, too, was the only child born of my mother and father's love," Wolf Hawk said. He smiled into her eyes when she saw surprise leap into them. "You see, my mother was not strong. She gave birth to me, then died shortly after. My father never married again."

"My parents were everything to me," Mia murmured.

"They are gone, so I will be that everything now, my woman," Wolf Hawk said, then swept both arms beneath her and brought her lips to his again with savage abandon.

Mia was not certain how it happened, but suddenly she realized that they both were unclothed.

His naked body pressed against hers, and she felt the full length of his manhood as he guided it with his hand between her legs. He pressed it against her opening, where she only now realized that she was wet and ready for his entrance.

She had never seen a man unclothed before, even though the spaces on the scow were small and did not give one much room for privacy. She could not help being dismayed by the size of Wolf Hawk's manhood as it pressed against her flesh. Its warm touch made her feel oddly giddy.

"Open more widely to me," Wolf Hawk whispered into her ear. "It is time for us to make love. I will be gentle. I want you to remember this first time as one of much pleasure."

Having no idea what to expect when he went all the way inside her, and being somewhat afraid, since he seemed so big and she was so petite, Mia felt her pulse race.

If not for that strange yearning inside her, she might even change her mind about making love, but her heart seemed to cry out for their complete togetherness.

Wolf Hawk realized how tentative she now was about what they were doing, and he understood. The first time for a woman, especially a woman as sweet and as inexperienced as Mia, could be frightening.

"I shall kiss you and hold you in my arms as I

go further inside you," he whispered into her ear, holding her tenderly against him. "There will be some pain, but with me the pain will be very brief and I will then take you with me to a place that will make you cry out with pleasure."

Trying to ready herself for that moment of pain Wolf Hawk had prepared her for, Mia lay stiffly, her mind no longer filled with ecstasy but fear. She clung to him as he tenderly nudged her legs farther apart.

She closed her eyes as he slowly shoved his heat within her. To her surprise, she was filled with desire all over again when Wolf Hawk held her tightly against him and kissed her.

She did feel a pang of pain when he went even farther into her, but then realized it was true what he had said about pleasure coming after pain. As he began his rhythmic strokes inside her, now thrusting deeply, ecstasy rose up in her.

Her eyes pooled with tears of joy as he leaned down and showered her breasts with sweet kisses, then stopped at one of the breasts and drew its nipple gently between his teeth to nibble on it.

Never had she known such things happened between a man and a woman, that a breast could be worshipped by a man as Wolf Hawk was now doing. He cupped one of hers so gently in his hand, as his tongue sent pleasure throughout her.

She felt a splendid joy when his lips came to hers again and kissed her hungrily. She knew now to move her body with his, in order to deepen the pleasure that was filling her.

Wolf Hawk enfolded her in his solid strength as he held her. Their togetherness, their lovemaking, stoked fires within him that he had never felt before.

But he had never been in love before. He had never known a woman like Mia before.

Ho, the Winnebago women were beautiful and desirable, but there was something about Mia that made him know she was born to be his, no matter the color of the skin. In her heart she was Winnebago.

Theirs was a union that had been blessed by not only his Earthmaker, but also her own god.

"I want you as mine forever," he whispered against her lips as he paused for a moment before taking her on to paradise with him. "I want you as my wife."

Mia's eyes clouded with doubt for a moment. "But will your people accept me?"

"They already have," Wolf Hawk said, searching her eyes. "Will you be my wife?"

"You know that I will," Mia said, smiling sweetly at him.

Everything within him sang and soared as Wolf Hawk smiled back at her.

"Soon, my woman," he said huskily. "Very soon we will be blessed by both our gods as husband and wife."

"I already feel that we have been," Mia murmured.

"My woman, my love," Wolf Hawk said, then kissed her with a heat that was new to her, yet welcomed.

Fiercely, he drew her even closer. He thrust into her as their lips met again in trembling kisses.

And then as they clung and made love, Mia felt something so wonderfully blissful, she knew that she had just experienced the ultimate of pleasure. The wondrous feeling seemed never to stop as he continued with his thrusts, and then moaned as his body quivered and quaked against hers.

Slowly they came down from the clouds of rapture, lying together beside the slowly burning embers of the fire, their bodies still touching, their hands clasped. Mia closed her eyes and smiled.

"I never knew such wondrous feelings could exist between a man and a woman," she murmured.

She opened her eyes, turned on her side to face Wolf Hawk, and ran a hand slowly over his powerfully muscled chest. Then she dared to move her hand lower, where he was no longer as large, yet still large enough to amaze her at his greatness.

"A man is so different from a woman," she said, smiling into his eyes as she moved her hand away from him. "I'm glad I don't have something like that to deal with every day as I walk around in my clothes."

She lifted an eyebrow. "How can you get . . . get . . . yourself arranged in your clothes so that it is not uncomfortable every time you move?" she asked.

She blushed when he laughed good-naturedly and took her hand to lay it on his manhood.

"This that you think might be a bother is a source of pride to every man. If it is large, he is glad that it will give pleasure to the woman he loves," he said. "I, personally, never feel it is an intrusion in my life."

He enfolded his manhood with her hand. "Move your hand on me and see what happens," he said, already feeling the renewed pleasure her hand was causing.

Mia blushed, for this was all new to her. Even this morning before Wolf Hawk had taken her in his arms, she never would have believed this could happen.

But there they were, as intimate as a man and woman could be, and she was actually not embarrassed by it.

It seemed the right thing to do. They were meant for each other.

Her eyes widened when she saw the effect her hands were having. His manhood was actually growing right before her eyes and she could hear him breathing heavily.

His pleasure was evident as she gazed into his eyes. She saw there a sort of haziness that seemed to come with sexual excitement.

Unable to take much more without spilling his seed right into her palm, Wolf Hawk took her hand away from him.

He rolled her beneath him, wrapped her within his muscled arms and again pushed himself into her waiting folds. He lifted her legs up around him so that he could fill her more deeply, and they came together in a passionately hot kiss.

Mia was surprised that it was possible to make love a second time so soon. But already ecstasy was building in her again with bone-weakening intensity.

With a moan of ecstasy she clung to him as he kissed her and thrust eagerly inside her over and over again. This time it did not take as long for them to reach the peak of pleasure.

Paradise reached, their bodies became still, and suddenly again, as earlier, the earth seemed to move and rock beneath them. Mia knew it had nothing to do with what they had just shared a second time this morning.

Wolf Hawk eased away from her.

He reached for her.

They both quickly dressed themselves, yet the ground beneath the floor mats was quiet and calm again.

"What does it mean?" Mia asked, searching his eyes as she combed her fingers through her hair.

"It seems that Earthmaker is angry at someone," Wolf Hawk said.

He reached a hand out for Mia, taking it and walking with her to the closed entrance flap.

He untied the thongs that had held the flap shut so that they had privacy, then grabbed Mia when the earth shook again, this time, more fiercely.

"I'm afraid," Mia said, clutching him.

"When you are with me, you never need to be

afraid. I will protect you, always, from harm," Wolf Hawk said in his deep voice, but he knew that something was truly awry.

He wondered if his grandfather had anything to do with it? He knew that Talking Bird could cause many things to happen if he were angry about something.

But if it was his grandfather who was willing this to happen, he knew that all would be well for his people. Talking Bird would never do anything that could bring harm to their Bird Clan.

Wolf Hawk and Mia walked outside together. They looked all around them.

Several women had come from their lodges, clutching their children's hands. But there was no obvious wreckage among the lodges of the village.

Several people came to Wolf Hawk, their eyes wide with wonder.

"All is well," he said, gently placing a hand on a small girl's head. "You women may resume your daily chores. The children may go back to their play."

He looked over at several of his elders who were sitting beside a large outdoor fire. They did not seem perturbed by nature's teasing.

These elders were the wisest of all of his Bird Clan except for his Shaman grandfather. Wolf Hawk noticed that several of them seemed to be watching the river.

Mia's eyes followed Wolf Hawk's. He was look-ing with concern toward Shadow Island, which was hidden from sight by the same low-hanging fog that Mia saw there so often.

She gazed up at Wolf Hawk, but said nothing, only waited . . .

Chapter Twenty-five

I will have my revenge,
I will have it if I die
The moment after.

—Spanish Curate

A small longboat was making its way down the Rush River. The name MIA painted on both sides of the boat revealed who the true owner was, yet it was two men who eagerly drew their paddles through the water.

"We cain't be all that far away now, Jeb," Clint said as he squinted against the sun and looked along the shore for the first signs of the rocky beach that fronted the dilapidated fort.

"I think it was asinine coming back here so soon," Jeb growled out. "And what the hell is going on? Did you see those waves that came out of nowhere a short while ago? Did you see some of the trees swaying on shore? If I didn't know better, I'd think we just experienced an earthquake. If so, we're damn lucky."

"Yeah, it's kinda spooky, if you ask me," Clint said. He looked over his shoulder and then straight ahead.

"I think we should turn around and go back to St. Louis," Jeb said nervously. "We were almost there and then you get the stupid idea of comin' back for the pelts before I know we should. I'm afraid what we just experienced, the water shaking and all, is a warning of some sort from those two young braves' spirits."

He visibly shuddered. "I can feel 'em even now, all around me," he said. "I'll never forget the look on their faces and their death stares as we came upon them in the traps.

"We should've took 'em outta those traps and carried them far away and hid 'em, or just dropped their bodies in the river where no one'd ever find them," Jeb grumbled. "But no. We left 'em there for their people to find. Surely even now revenge lies heavy on those people's hearts. If they catch us comin' back here to get those pelts, it'll be our scalps that'll be hangin' on scalp poles."

"Oh, shut up," Clint snapped, his eyes narrowing with anger. "Just keep that paddle goin'. We'll get those pelts and head back to St. Louis. No one'll ever be the wiser that we came here again. Those Injuns don't have eyes in the backs of their heads and they sure enough had no idea the pelts were hidden at the fort."

"I'd just feel better if we'd stayed headed for St. Louis, not here," Jeb said. "But now that we are almost at the fort, let's get it done and over with. Work harder with that paddle, Clint."

"The dumb savages," Clint said, laughing throatily. "They had a treasure so close at hand and never knew it."

"My one regret is abandoning that scow," Jeb

mumbled. "Once we reached St. Louis we could've got a pretty penny for that thing. Now? It's just sitting there where we left it onshore for anyone to come and take, free and clear of any cost."

"Just stop your bitchin'," Clint said. "Sometimes I think I've got a woman as my companion, not a man. Bitch, bitch, bitch. That's all you do anymore."

"Look!" Jeb said, stopping and using his paddle to point out a part of the land that he recognized. "See that? Don't you recognize that huge pile of rock? I remember it sits close to the fort. I figure some Englishman and Frenchman built that as a marker to those who might be trying to find the fort."

"Yep, I see it, we're almost there," Clint said. "I'm just about droolin' when I think on all of those pelts we're gonna rescue and take to St. Louie. Think of the money, Jeb. Jist think of the money we're gonna get from those pelts."

Suddenly Jeb cried out with fear, his eyes widened when the water began to thrash, tossing the boat from side to side.

"Lord, Jeb, what's happening?" Clint cried as he dropped the paddle to the bottom of the boat so that he could cling to the sides with all his might.

He gazed heavenward and gasped when he saw geese screeching overhead and scattering in all directions. Then he cried out in fear as he watched the riverbanks quiver and shake. Fish leapt from the heaving water.

"We're gonna die!" Jeb screamed as the river-banks began to crumble and cave in, tumbling into the water.

Then suddenly everything became strangely still.

All of the crazed movements ceased.

Clint and Jeb, whose hearts were pounding wildly in their chests, watched as whole chunks of the banks along the river now tumbled into the water. The splash was so fierce on both sides of the river, both Clint and Jeb became afraid that the boat might capsize.

"Look yonder, Jeb," Clint cried as a slow mist rose heavenward, revealing an island not far away from where they sat totally terrified. "It's like the good Lord above placed it there for us to find safety from what might happen next. It seems un-touched by the earthquake."

"Let's go," Jeb said, already paddling toward it. Reluctantly, Clint began helping him. He recalled having seen this strange mist before and wonder-ing what might be hiding beneath it.

Now that he saw the island, a chill rode his spine. He had the strangest feeling that there was something mystical about how the mist had just suddenly opened up to him and Jeb, revealing an island that they'd had no idea was there.

"Why now?" he whispered to himself.

Then he shrugged.

Surely the earthquake had caused the mist to lift away from the ground. What else could it truly be?

But there was one thing that still troubled him.

He knew that this mist he had seen before was not far from the Winnebago village.

"I don't think we should go there," Clint suddenly said, lifting his paddle from the water. "Come on, Jeb. Let's get the boat turned around and hightail it outta here while we have the chance. I don't trust what's happened here today. None of it. Maybe those Winnebago Injuns have strange mystical powers white people don't."

"Clint, stop your whinin' and remember what we just went through," Jeb grumbled. "If the earthquake happens again and we're still in the river, we're doomed. Do you hear? Doomed."

"I just don't know," Clint said.

"Put that damn paddle back in the water and row, damn it," Jeb snarled. He gave Clint a look that went right through him. "Let's get on dry land. I'll feel way safer there than on the water. Another earthquake could capsize our boat quicker than you can blink your eyes."

"Oh, alright," Clint said, sliding his paddle back into the water and taking up the same rhythm as Jeb.

"Everything is too quiet," Jeb said, looking cautiously at the island as they got closer to it. "I hear no birds singing. Nothin'. It's like everything is dead."

"Just like we'll be if we stay in this water for much longer," Jeb said.

He leapt from the boat when he realized that he

could stand on the bottom of the river, and grunted as he began dragging the boat closer to shore.

"Get outta there and lend me a hand, Clint," Jeb snapped. "Now. Do you hear? Now!"

Clint looked guardedly past Jeb, at the thick vegetation of the island. He recognized a clump of wolf willows, which he had never known existed until they had come to this part of Minnesota.

Yep, he knew for certain that he and Jeb were much too close to Injun territory, for he had seen wolf willows before when they were trying to escape through the forest. He now associated those trees with the Winnebago, and . . . trouble!

Finally onshore, both Jeb and Clint hauled the boat up on a rock that would keep it from floating away.

"This certainly ain't what I figured we'd be doin' about now," Clint growled out as he stood with Jeb, gazing with troubled eyes toward the thickness of the trees that lay before them.

"Bein' here is askin' for trouble." Clint grumbled. "We're the same as givin' the Injuns an invite to come and take us back to their village. I've heard it said that they tie their prisoners to stakes, even light fires and let their captives die slowly in the flames."

"Just shut up, Clint," Jeb said. "We have no choice but to seek shelter here for a while. Once we know the river is safe to travel on, we'll leave. Then we'll find a good place to hide. The Injuns won't know the difference."

"We should've hid the boat," Clint said, looking over his shoulder toward where they had left the boat beached. "That's all we need . . . Injuns seein' the boat. They'll find us. For sure they'll find us."

Jeb stopped dead in his tracks. "You're right," he suddenly said. "It seems there is no more threat of an earthquake." He looked slowly around him. "See how things seem to have calmed? Even the birds are singing again."

"Then let's get the hell outta here," Clint said. "I don't know what we were thinkin'. Even before we beached the canoe, the water had become calm. Hurry. Let's get back to the boat, go to the fort, and get the hell away from this spooky place."

They broke into a mad run and soon reached the boat. Panting hard, they shoved it back in the water.

They boarded it, grabbed up the paddles, and huffing and puffing hard, they rowed as quickly as possible toward the pile of rocks that marked the fort.

They could almost feel the plushness of the furs against their fingers.

"Oh, Lordie, no, not again!" Jeb cried, dropping the paddle to the bottom of the boat and clinging to the sides for dear life as sudden waves began thrashing the boat from side to side.

They again saw trees swaying on the shore, and sections of shoreline breaking away and settling in the water.

"The island!" Clint screamed as he rowed back

in its direction. "Jeb, we've got to get back to the island or die in this damn river."

They beached the boat again and this time didn't hesitate to run straight into the wolf willows!

Chapter Twenty-six

No soul can ever clearly see
Another highest, noblest part,
Save through the sweet philosophy,
And loving wisdom of the heart.

—Phoebe Cary

Mia stood as though in shock as she looked past the village tepees and into the forest just beyond. She saw several fallen trees and even some cracks in the land.

This latest quake, which had occurred only moments ago, had frightened her so much she couldn't move or even cry out.

Miracle of miracles, nothing in the village had been damaged. She saw some women clinging to their children's hands while others ran to their warrior husbands. It was obvious that they were no less afraid than she.

She looked up at Wolf Hawk. "Wolf Hawk, I don't understand," Mia managed to say, her voice quavering. "There was an earthquake beyond the village, but not here. How can that happen?"

She looked toward the river. She had seen the water splashing violently. She had even seen chunks of earth breaking away from the shoreline and falling into it.

Now she looked into the middle of the river and saw Shadow Island clearly for the first time. The usual mist that hung over it had lifted.

She looked quickly up at Wolf Hawk again and saw that his own eyes were on the island.

"Do you think your grandfather was harmed?" Mia asked, remembering her time with Talking Bird.

Such a kind man.

Oh, but surely his Earthmaker wouldn't have allowed anything to happen to him. He was on this earth for a purpose . . . a good one.

Wolf Hawk knew for certain that his elderly grandfather had not been harmed, for it surely had been Talking Bird who had willed the earthquake to happen.

But Wolf Hawk could not imagine why he had done so. His grandfather rarely used his magic in such a forceful way, unless . . .

He took Mia's hands. "I must go and see how he is," he said thickly.

"Can I go with you?" Mia asked, searching his eyes.

"No, you stay," Wolf Hawk said. He reached a gentle hand to her cheek. "I shall not be long."

She nodded, yet leaned into his hand the brief moment it was there.

"All is well, my people," he said, looking from one to the other. "Again, as before when the earth has shaken and the river has foamed up from the turmoil of a quake, we have been spared. Go on about your work. I am going to check on my grandfather."

He nodded at one warrior and then another. "Go into the forest and gather wood from those trees that were felled by nature's wrath," he said. "Fill the gaps in the ground with some of the fallen debris. We do not want such things left unattended."

He looked from child to child. "You stay with your mothers," he said lovingly. "Do not stray beyond our village, for danger lies there until your fathers correct it."

The children seemed to nod in unison, their eyes wide as they gazed back at their chief, who was even more respected than even their fathers or mothers. Chief Wolf Hawk was everything to this Winnebago clan.

"I will leave now," Wolf Hawk said. "Go. You all have your own duties to tend to."

At that, the people disbanded.

Wolf Hawk watched several warriors leave the village, then he turned to Mia again. "I will not be long," he said. "Go inside my lodge. The fear you felt will soon dissipate, like the earthquake, itself."

"I will," Mia murmured. "I hope you find your grandfather well."

"He is a strong man who has overcome many obstacles that stood in his way during his lifetime," Wolf Hawk said. "So shall he survive this."

He ached to draw Mia into his arms and hold

her, but knew that until he announced their upcoming marriage, he must practice restraint in front of his people.

But soon?

Ho, soon they would be able to reveal their love for each other to all.

He knew that some would doubt his sanity for having chosen a white woman over one of his own skin color. But he believed that, in time, even those people would see the goodness in Mia, just as Wolf Hawk had seen it.

"I truly must go now," he said, then turned and ran toward the river.

Mia watched him for a while longer, then went inside his tepee. She sat down beside the slow burning embers of the fire and became lost in thought.

She hoped that Wolf Hawk would return soon with good news about Talking Bird.

Because of the way he had helped her, she had developed a strange sort of attachment to the old shaman. She had told Wolf Hawk as much.

He had smiled and said that was the way of Talking Bird; everyone trusted and loved him.

Her eyebrows rose as her thoughts returned to Wolf Hawk. As she had watched him run toward the river, he had disappeared from view when he'd reached a small stand of trees.

From thereon she hadn't seen him, not even when she would have thought that he would be in the river in a canoe, headed for the island. He just seemed suddenly gone!

She felt a slight shiver ride her spine at that thought.

She recalled again how he had seemed to have materialized out of nowhere, appearing from a patch of fog.

She could not help believing that there were many things about Wolf Hawk that she might never know, or understand.

But she did know that she could not live without him. He was now everything to her. And soon she would be his wife!

She frowned a little. Not because she had agreed to be his wife, but because she feared his people's reactions to the news.

If they didn't approve of her, what then? Would Wolf Hawk feel that he must turn his back on her because his first duty was to his people?

She shook her head to clear it. She would not let anything spoil the joy of those precious moments before the earth had begun to shake beneath them.

She smiled. For a moment she had thought that their lovemaking had had a strange effect on her, making her feel as though the earth itself was shaking.

"I must get hold of myself," she said out loud, then glanced at the birdcage where Georgina was sitting silently on her perch. Surely the canary had been frightened by the earthquake.

She went to the cage and smiled at Georgina. "Do not be afraid," she murmured. "All is well, sweet thing. You can sing now. I wish that you would. It would lighten my mood."

As though the bird understood her, Georgina began her beautiful warbling as she slowly strutted along the perch.

"Thank you, sweet bird," Mia murmured, going back and sitting down by the fire.

She looked slowly around Wolf Hawk's tepee.

She could still feel him there, even while he was gone. She felt so blessed to have been brought into his life. She could not believe that she was going to become his wife.

She thought about how so much had changed in her life in such a short time. She had always wondered about her future, whether or not she would find a man to love, and who would love her in return.

And she had! She was going to be living a life that she would have never imagined possible, for she would be living it in an Indian village with an Indian husband . . . Wolf Hawk!

Oh, but she did so badly want to become Wolf Hawk's woman and have a home of her own.

And now she would have it all.

Her life wouldn't be anything like she had imagined it would be previously. She was not going to live in a house or in a town.

She was going to be living in a tepee in an Indian village.

"With Wolf Hawk!" she said aloud, smiling at how lucky she was to have been rescued by him, even though at first she had been brought to his village as Wolf Hawk's captive!

"I am still a captive," she whispered, smiling at

Georgina as she continued to sing. "A captive to the love of a wonderful man!"

She could not believe this was happening to her. It was like stories she had read about knights and beautiful ladies finding one another.

"I have found my true knight," she whispered, giggling at the comparison of Wolf Hawk to a knight.

The thought of marrying Wolf Hawk was much more romantic and exciting than marrying a knight could ever be. Was not Wolf Hawk a great, powerful chief, the king of the forest?

"Listen to me," Mia said to Georgina. "I have suddenly gone daft!"

She smiled and again gazed into the flames of the fire.

Something deep inside told her that Talking Bird was alright, which gave her the right to think about frivolous things such as knights.

She just hoped that Wolf Hawk would return soon.

If there were another earthquake, this time it might consume the entire Indian village. As quickly as that her dreams . . . her hopes . . . her desires . . . would be dashed.

Her future with Wolf Hawk would only be an impossible dream.

Chapter Twenty-seven

The winds of heaven mix forever,
With a sweet emotion.

— *Shelley*

Desperately clutching their rifles, Jeb and Clint walked cautiously through the forest on the mysterious island. They both hoped they would be safe there, at least for awhile until the danger of another earthquake was past.

"How can this island be untouched by the earthquake?" Clint mumbled as he looked cautiously around him, through a hazy sort of mist, then straight ahead again. "I'm afraid it's some sort of witchcraft voodoo something or other that's happening here."

He looked over at Jeb. "Don'tcha feel it, Jeb?" he asked. He hunched his shoulders with fear now as the mist seemed to be slowly enveloping them.

"Stop thinkin' up trouble," Jeb grumbled. "Let's jist find us a place to rest awhile until we're sure there won't be another quake. Then we'll go and get those pelts and hightail it outta here."

"Everything is calm now, so why not try leaving again?" Clint whined. "Like I said, this here island is spooky as hell. And you know it lays just across the river from that Injun village. That alone makes me shake in my boots. What if one of those Injuns seen us beach the boat on the island? Don'tcha think they might put two and two together and figure out that we're the ones responsible for the two braves' deaths?"

"I'm sure they're as spooked about the quake as we are, so they won't be comin' to see what's happening on this island," Jeb said. "And let's not borrow trouble by thinkin' on Injuns at a time when we need to just be thinkin' on gettin' outta here as soon as we feel it's safe."

Jeb flinched when he heard a loud whirring above him. He looked quickly up. "Clint!" he cried, stiffening. "Look above you. In the break of the trees where we can see the sky. Didja see that large hawk? Lordie be, it's the same bird I saw before. Did you hear the noise those wings made?"

Clint looked up at the sky and saw nothing, then gave Jeb a sour glance. "You're lettin' your imagination run wild," he snapped. "Stop borrowing trouble, do you hear?"

"But I seen it, Clint," Jeb snapped angrily. "And I heard it. How could you not have seen and heard the same thing? You're right beside me."

"If you saw such a big bird, where is it now?" Clint demanded. "Look up there. The sky is clear not only of birds, but clouds. I'd say our worries are almost over. Soon we'll be in the boat on our way back to St. Louie, where we'll be rich men once we sell those pelts. Lordie be, Jeb. Those are some of the richest, finest pelts we've gathered up in years. The fox is prime fur. Them alone will make us set for life."

Jeb scarcely heard what Clint was saying. He was still confused by how the huge hawk could be there one minute and gone the next. It was as though someone or something had plucked it from the sky.

Then he jumped in alarm when he saw something else up ahead. It was a wolf bounding through the trees away from them.

What frightened him the most was the thought that where there was one wolf, there was usually a pack.

He looked on both sides of him, and then over his shoulder, but when he saw no signs of any other wolves, he again focused straight ahead on the one he did see. It still ran onward, apparently having not realized that Clint and Jeb were so close.

And then Jeb stopped dead in his tracks. Were his eyes playing tricks on him? He thought he saw the wolf suddenly change into a muscled, scarcely clothed Indian!

Jeb reached out for Clint. He had stopped behind him, his eyes wide with fear.

In desperation, Jeb grabbed hold of one of Clint's arms. "Clint, you can't tell me that you didn't see what I just saw," he said. He gulped hard. "How can it be? How . . . can . . . a wolf . . . change into a man? And . . . and . . . I'd bet my last dollar that the hawk I saw . . . changed into that wolf!"

"This has to be a haunted island or something,"

Clint said, coming out of his own fearful amazement. He slapped Jeb's hand from his arm. "And that Injun up there surely lives on this island."

He blinked his eyes and then rubbed them, but when he looked ahead again, he still saw the Indian. The warrior was running somewhere mighty fast, thankfully away from him and Jeb.

"I don't know what's goin' on here but I do know one thing," Jeb said, already turning and running toward the river. "I'm gettin' off this island as fast as my legs will carry me to the boat. Come on, Clint. Let's get away from this place before someone turns us into toads."

As Clint ran beside Jeb, he wanted to laugh at Jeb's joke about toads, but he was too terrified. He had always heard that Indians practiced witchcraft, but this took the cake! He just had to forget about having seen it or else he might lose his mind. What they had witnessed just didn't happen.

Yes, it had to have been a figment of both his and Jeb's imagination!

Clint's knees were weak with fear. Suddenly they buckled beneath him and he fell into a thick clump of bushes, crying out when thorns pierced his breeches and stabbed him in his legs.

"Good Lord, Clint," Jeb said, stopping and reaching down to help his partner up. "Now's not the time to be a big baby. Come on. We've got to get to that boat."

Wolf Hawk stopped dead in his tracks when Clint's yelp of pain carried to him on the wind.

He turned and saw two men, one on the ground, the other reaching a helping hand to him.

Wolf Hawk had been too focused on getting to his grandfather to have heard the intruders on Shadow Island. He supposed they had sought shelter on the island from the earthquake.

That had been their first mistake.

The second was allowing Wolf Hawk to know they were there.

No white man was welcome on his grandfather's island, now . . . or ever.

Before Jeb could cock his rifle, Wolf Hawk was there, taking the weapon away from him.

Clint struggled to his feet, his eyes wide with fear. He would never forget the terrifying sight of the wolf changing into this Indian.

He knew that it hadn't been his imagination, yet how could it have been real? All he knew was that Indians were capable of mysterious things, and that was frightening.

Wolf Hawk wasn't certain if these men had seen his transformations. If they had, he could not allow them to spread the news to others. Yet he was not a man of violence. He did not wish to kill them.

Suddenly he recognized the amulet necklace that hung around the one man's neck, and Wolf Hawk knew to whom it had belonged.

These were the very men who were responsible for the deaths of the two braves.

He could only conclude they had brazenly returned to Winnebago land to get the pelts they had left behind.

But Wolf Hawk didn't immediately accuse them of the deaths. He would think through just how they should pay for their crime.

He realized now that Talking Bird must have known the two trappers had returned to this area. He had purposely caused the earthquakes to force them to seek safety on the island.

Talking Bird most certainly had the power to do this. He could do all sorts of magical things that no one would ever believe.

But Wolf Hawk knew. And he understood, for Wolf Hawk was a part of the old Shaman's magic.

Wolf Hawk decided to play a mind game with these two men before taking his final vengeance against them.

He acted as though he had no idea who they were.

"Why are you on this island?" Wolf Hawk asked, his eyes moving from one to the other.

It gave him much pleasure to see their fear. He wanted to laugh out loud at them, but if he did, they would know that they were definitely in the presence of their enemy.

Clint stood beside Jeb now. They exchanged nervous, troubled glances.

"We were on our way to St. Louis," Clint said, his voice thin with fear, for something told him that this Indian was toying with him and Jeb. But he continued with his lie, fabricating it as he went along. He just hoped that he sounded convincing.

"Our . . . wives . . . went ahead of us," he said. "They are waiting even now for us."

Astute as he was, Wolf Hawk could always tell when someone was lying. As the man talked, his eyes had not rested, jerking from side to side. And both men were shifting uneasily from one foot to the other.

Ho, the man was lying and Wolf Hawk now knew for certain that these men had returned for the pelts that had been left hidden at the fort.

To pull these men more deeply into the game that Wolf Hawk was playing with them, he suddenly handed the rifle back to the man he had taken it from. It was safe to do this, for he knew that he was no longer alone with the men.

He felt the presence of Talking Bird behind him, hidden from the view of the two men. Talking Bird would not allow them to get the better of Wolf Hawk.

He saw the amazement in the man's eyes as he took the rifle back from Wolf Hawk. Clint's hand trembled as he took possession of the rifle, for he felt that something was very wrong. No Indian would trust a white man enough to hand him back the means to kill him.

Unless . . .

"The earthquake is over," Wolf Hawk said, looking slowly from one man to the other. "The waters are calm. Go now. Go in peace."

Clint and Jeb exchanged wary glances, not knowing what to believe.

"Are you serious?" Jeb asked, while Clint gave him a burning glance for asking such a foolish question.

"You can go," Wolf Hawk repeated.

Clint gripped his rifle hard. "Thank you," he said thickly.

He turned quickly, and with Jeb running beside him, they hurried to the boat. In a matter of minutes they had it out in the water and were quickly paddling back toward the fort.

Wolf Hawk smiled cunningly and allowed them time enough to get to the fort. Then he would prove to them how wrong they were to put trust in someone who despised the very ground they walked on.

He remembered the amulet hanging around the one man's neck. He did not want to even think about the moment the man had taken it from Little Bull. It had been a sacrilegious thing to do, and that man would be the first to pay for his crime.

"White men, enjoy your last moments of life," Wolf Hawk whispered to himself.

Chapter Twenty-eight

I'll tell you how the sun rose—
A ribbon at a time.

—Dickinson

Wolf Hawk turned and smiled at Talking Bird. He hurried to him and gently embraced him, then stepped away.

"It is good to see that you came through the earthquakes so well," Wolf Hawk said. He walked now beside his grandfather as they headed back to the old Shaman's tepee. "Of course I knew that you would."

They walked onward with wolf willows on both sides of them. "We were untouched, as well, at the village, yet there were many trees beyond that were felled by the energy of the quakes," he said. "Also some of the banks of the river were disturbed. Otherwise, all is well."

They walked in silence now as the songbirds in the trees serenaded them, and both relished this moment of peace.

When they reached Talking Bird's tepee, he stopped and turned to Wolf Hawk. "You were good to come," he said thickly. "But your Shaman grandfather is alright. You need not stay when you have more important things to do."

"*Ho*, I do," Wolf Hawk said gravely.

He looked over his shoulder, in the direction that the trappers had disappeared.

In his mind's eye he again saw the hunting amulet that the one man wore.

Wolf Hawk would soon remove the amulet from around the trapper's neck.

He would take it to Little Bull's mother. She would then have a part of her son with her again.

"Those two men that you saw with me?" Wolf Hawk said, again gazing at his grandfather. "They are guilty of having set the traps that killed our two young braves. I am giving them false hope by allowing them to go on their way. But soon they will know that my kindness was only a ploy. I will soon have vengeance against them."

Talking Bird smiled. He reached a wrinkled hand to Wolf Hawk's bare shoulder and rested it there as he spoke. "I know who they are," he said, nodding. "In my wisdom I knew they were in the water near our people's homes again. I purposely caused the earthquakes to disrupt the white men's plans, and to put terror into their hearts. I made certain that what I did with my powers did not bring harm to our people.

"Go now, my grandson," Talking Bird then said, lowering his hand away from Wolf Hawk and dropping it slowly to his own side. "Follow through with your plan. You will find the men at the abandoned fort. That is where you can complete your vengeance. My role is over."

Wolf Hawk embraced Talking Bird again, then

as Talking Bird proudly watched, Wolf Hawk transformed himself into the hawk, and with his huge outspreading wings, flew up and through the wolf willows.

When Wolf Hawk reached the sky in his hawk form, he soared onward, his bold, wide eyes ever watching down below, until he saw the beached boat at the riverbank close to the fort. He dove downward, his wings causing a huge shadow below him.

When he reached the ground, he landed and once again became a man. His jaw tight with determination, his heart pounding at the thought of finally making these two men pay for their misjudgments in life, he ran toward the entrance of the fort.

He stopped momentarily and smiled when he heard sudden loud wails of despair. He knew what had caused them. The trappers had just discovered that the pelts were gone.

He ran to the cabin where his warriors had discovered the hidden furs.

When he stepped inside the door, the trappers turned pale at the sight of him. They had left him on the island, yet there had been no sign of a canoe. They must be wondering how Wolf Hawk had gotten there from his village.

Surely it had not taken long for them to guess why Wolf Hawk had not needed a canoe. Both men had no doubt seen Wolf Hawk change from a huge, powerful hawk to a wolf, and then soon after, to a man.

Ho, he could see in their wide, frightened eyes that they were wondering what other mystical powers Wolf Hawk might have. They both held rifles, but were obviously too afraid to use them.

Wolf Hawk stepped up to them. With each of his hands he grabbed the rifles from the men.

"Please don't harm us," both men said in unison.

"Please have mercy," Clint begged, his voice filled with a whining that sent disgust through Wolf Hawk. To him, a man who whined like an unhappy puppy was not a man at all.

"Let us go," Jeb cried, tears filling his eyes. "We promise never to come back. We just want to go away from this place and forget we were ever here. It's a . . . crazy . . . place, filled with mystery and things I don't want even to believe I saw."

Wolf Hawk did not respond verbally to what either of them said. Instead he took one rifle at a time and removed the ammunition, tossing the firearms over his shoulder.

"You must come with me now," Wolf Hawk then said, beckoning to them with an outstretched hand.

"Why?" Jeb gasped, unable to control the trembling of his entire body. "What do you want with us?"

"Do you truly need to ask?" Wolf Hawk said bitterly. "You must know what you are guilty of, or else why did you flee? You should never have returned, yet it was willed by my grandfather that you would."

"Your . . . grandfather . . . ?" Clint asked, his eyes widening.

"My Shaman grandfather knows all things," Wolf Hawk said, slowly smiling. "He willed you to return to Winnebago land. When he knew you had arrived, he spoke and the river was filled with rage, the same rage I felt that day when I found my people's two young braves dead in your claws of death."

Wolf Hawk paused, looked slowly from one to the other, then said, "He commanded, too, that the land on each side of the river would break away. How did you ever think that you could come again as though nothing had happened and claim the pelts and take them away?"

"We meant no one harm; we did not mean to kill those two young braves," Jeb whined. "It . . . just . . . happened."

"As it just happened that one of you took the hunting amulet from Little Bull as he lay dead in a pool of his own life's blood?" Wolf Hawk demanded, gazing intently at the amulet that now hung around Jeb's neck.

Wolf Hawk left it there for now, but soon it would be taken back to the mother of its rightful owner.

First he wanted everyone to see the proof of who these men were. The amulet conclusively proved that these trappers were responsible for the boys' deaths.

Clint glared at Jeb. "I told you that you shouldn't take that amulet," he growled out.

Jeb lowered his eyes and swallowed hard, then winced when Wolf Hawk grabbed him by the arm and yanked him from the cabin. Clint walked shakily beside him.

"Please, oh, please let us go," Jeb cried. "We truly meant those young men no harm."

Wolf Hawk stopped and glared at him. "I am taking you to the mother of the two braves who died in your deadly traps, so that she will see who took her sons' lives," he said coldly.

"Please, no," Clint cried. "Why cain't you listen to reason? We didn't mean for any of that to happen. Please let us go. We promise, oh, Lord, we promise never to come to Winnebago land again. And we won't tell anyone about you and how you treated us. We promise."

Those words only antagonized Wolf Hawk even more. So far, he had not treated the men badly at all.

"Come," Wolf Hawk said, shoving first one man, and then the other, out of the cabin. "Your words are wasted on me."

He kept shoving them until they finally reached the beached boat.

"Get in," Wolf Hawk commanded. "Now!"

Clint and Jeb fell all over each other as they scrambled to get in the boat. Wolf Hawk made them sit facing the seat he would take.

After Wolf Hawk got the boat in deeper water, he boarded it, himself. For a moment he just sat there, glaring at the men, wanting them to become as uncomfortable as possible. Then he lifted the paddle and started back in the direction of his village.

Jeb and Clint sat there, trembling, their eyes transfixed on Wolf Hawk. Both were afraid that he might turn suddenly into a bird or a wolf.

They had enough common sense left to realize that Wolf Hawk surely wouldn't allow them to live to tell others of the mystical happenings they had witnessed. They also knew that he was going to make them both pay for the deaths of those two young braves.

They just wondered how he would choose to take revenge. Would their deaths be slow, or mercifully fast? Either way, they were absolutely terrified.

Then it came to Jeb just how slowly the two young braves must have died. He was certain now that he and Clint would be made to die just as slowly and painfully.

"Please, oh, please reconsider," Jeb cried out. "Let us go!"

As before, Wolf Hawk ignored his pleadings.

He just continued paddling onward, his heart set on finally achieving the vengeance demanded by the mother of the two young braves. He was more than happy to do this for Dancing Fire.

Chapter Twenty-nine

Some fears, a soft regret,
For joys scarce known.

—*Barry Cornwall*

Mia heard a commotion outside of Wolf Hawk's tepee and then a strange sort of silence.

She had waited with an anxious heart for what seemed an eternity for Wolf Hawk's return. Now she wondered if what was happening in the village could be a sign that he had finally arrived.

Her pulse racing, she rose from where she had sat waiting for the man she loved, on thick pelts before the slow burning embers of the fire. Excitedly she hurried outside.

She stopped and gasped as she caught sight of Wolf Hawk beaching a boat with two men in it. Their faces were lined with fear as they gaped back at the staring Winnebago people who were gathering together now on the riverbank.

Mia was startled not only because Wolf Hawk was bringing two white men to the village, but also because he was paddling her family's longboat, with her very own name painted on both sides.

A sob lodged in her throat and she placed a hand over her mouth to stifle it when she recalled watching her father painting her name in bold white letters on the side of the boat. It had been a happy day in early spring. The sky had been filled with lovely white, fluffy clouds.

She had known that her father had already named the longboat after her, but he had taken forever to finally paint it on the boat. That was the way of her father. He had never done anything promptly, just took his time dawdling about his life, the pipe he loved so much usually clamped between his straight, white teeth.

That was why he had chosen to travel most summers on the river after having worked all winter making boats for other people. While floating idly from place to place on the scow he had no true responsibilities except to keep his family safe, happy, healthy and fed.

Yes, her father had done all of those things for his family, but Mia had lost her desire to travel on the water long before her father had decided to end their journey because of his health.

A thought came to her as she watched Wolf Hawk order the two men from the boat. Could these men be the trappers who had gotten away?

Had he somehow found them? Had they truly been foolish enough to return to the scene of the crime, thinking they could leave unmolested again with the pelts?

It surely was those two men. After all, they were aboard the longboat that had been stolen along with the scow.

They had to be the trappers who had brought

heartache into the lives of these Winnebago people and then fled on her family's scow.

Her jaw tight, her heart pounding, anger flaring in her eyes, she stepped farther from Wolf Hawk's tepee but did not approach the river. She didn't want to interfere in what must be done.

If these were truly the two men who were responsible for Little Bull's and Eagle Bear's deaths, surely Wolf Hawk would take the trappers to the braves' mother, so that she would see they had been captured and would be dealt with.

Mia stiffened when Wolf Hawk grabbed each of the men by an arm and walked them toward Mia. Why was he bringing them this way, she wondered.

She hoped the reason she was thinking was not true. Although he had said that he believed her story about the scow having been stolen, and that neither she nor her father had had anything to do with the trappers, it seemed he wanted to confirm her words.

Wolf Hawk stopped a few feet from her, shoving the trappers even closer. Was he going to ask them if they knew her?

A keen disappointment rushed through her to think that might be true. She had thought that she and Wolf Hawk trusted and loved each other.

But now? She was not all that certain.

Wolf Hawk turned to the two men. He looked from one to the other. "Do you see this young woman?" he demanded. "Ask her her name."

Mia's eyebrows rose at that question.

When neither man did as he was told, Wolf Hawk grabbed Clint by the throat. "Ask her," he said between clenched teeth.

"Ma'am, what . . . is . . . your name?" Clint stammered, trying to swallow as Wolf Hawk's fingers squeezed into his flesh.

"My name is Mia," she said softly.

"Mia?" Jeb gasped, recalling the name on both sides of the longboat. "The longboat we stole with the scow has the name Mia painted on it. Is that you?"

"The one and only," Mia said, her eyes flashing angrily into his. "You . . . men . . . are truly the cause of my father's death. You began it all by stealing the scow that he loved."

"How could that . . ." Clint began, but Wolf Hawk yanked him around and now walked him and Clint away from Mia.

Mia watched his people separate and make space for him to walk toward Dancing Fire, who stood stiffly just outside her lodge, listening and watching.

When Wolf Hawk finally got there, he gave both men a shove toward her. "This is the mother of the two braves your traps killed," he said.

The men tried to back away from Dancing Fire, whose accusing eyes were filled with angry tears. Her gaze immediately fixed on the hunting amulet that still hung around Jeb's neck. She gasped at the horror of seeing a white man, a murderer, wearing what had been so dear to her son Little Bull.

Wolf Hawk yanked it from Jeb's neck and handed it to Dancing Fire. He watched her fingers close around it. Then he stepped closer to her. "Dancing Fire, these are the two men who set the deadly traps," he said thickly. "They have today fallen into a trap of their own. They returned for the pelts that were no longer at the old fort. They are the guilty ones. They will now be made to pay for their crimes."

Wolf Hawk reached out and gently took one of Dancing Fire's hands in his. "Dancing Fire, how would you like to see justice served on these two men?" he asked softly. "What should be done to them?"

Dancing Fire said nothing, only sobbed.

He understood why she would not commit to saying how the men should pay for their crimes. Nothing could compensate her for the loss of her sons.

Wolf Hawk grabbed each man by an arm and again walked them toward Mia.

"Mia, how would you like to see these men pay for their crimes?" he asked thickly.

Mia's eyes wavered. She swallowed hard, then looked into Wolf Hawk's eyes. "It is not for me to say," she murmured. "Please do not leave it up to me. I'm just so glad that you found them. It ate away at my heart to know that those men who stole so much from me and your people were still out there, perhaps bringing more grief to someone else."

"I did not believe you would name a punishment, but I wanted to give you a chance," Wolf Hawk said quietly.

He turned to the men and looked from one to the other as they cowered beneath his angry stare.

"You came to this land to steal pelts?" he said. "You want pelts? I will take you now to where there will be many, but only from one type of animal. Wolves. You hid the pelts you claimed were yours at the old fort. We will go there again."

"Why . . . ?" Jeb managed to say, his voice thick with fear.

"You will soon see," Wolf Hawk said tightly. "As you will soon know your final fate."

Wolf Hawk turned to Mia and embraced her. "I will not be long," he said.

Mia nodded, then trembled as she watched Wolf Hawk shove both men in the direction of the river. She continued watching as he forced them into the longboat, then boarded it himself. Soon they were headed again toward the fort.

A chill rode her spine as she wondered what truly lay ahead for those two men.

Surely whatever Wolf Hawk had in mind would be merciful, for he was a man of peace, of love. Yet these men had wronged him and his people, as they had wronged Mia and her father.

Swallowing hard, Mia returned to Wolf Hawk's tepee. The people of the village resumed their daily activities, as though nothing had happened. Even Dancing Fire had returned to her own lodge, the amulet still clutched in one hand.

"Wolf Hawk, please, oh, please hurry back," Mia whispered as she settled again on the pelts beside the fire. She sighed and drew a blanket around her shoulders.

She looked occasionally toward the entrance flap as the wind rustled it. Then she turned her eyes again toward the fire, and watched the dancing flames, seeing in them all sorts of ghostly images.

Even Georgina sat quietly on her perch, her eyes watching Mia.

Chapter Thirty

Under the arch of life . . . I saw
Beauty enthroned; and though her gaze struck
*   awe,*
I drew it in as simply as my breath . . .
                                            —*Rossetti*

Mia looked toward the entrance flap, her heart skipping a beat when Wolf Hawk stepped inside. She got quickly to her feet and met him as he walked to her.

"You could not have gotten to the fort and still had time enough to come back to the village," Mia said, searching his eyes. "Why . . . have . . . you returned?"

Wolf Hawk took her hands in his. "Because of you," he said thickly. "I realized that you should go to the fort with me and the two trappers. I want you to witness what will happen."

"Truly?" Mia said, her eyes widening uncertainly. She looked past him, then into his eyes again. "Where are the trappers?"

"They are in the boat being guarded by one of my trusted warriors," Wolf Hawk said, now reaching a gentle hand out and taking one of hers. "Come with me now." He stopped and turned toward her. "But you must know that you will witness things that might frighten you. I ask that you do not let the things you see change your feelings toward me. Always remember that I am who I am, no matter what you might see."

"I . . . can't help being confused . . . and a little afraid," Mia murmured.

He drew her into his embrace. "Just know this, my woman," Wolf Hawk said softly. "I will always protect you and love you. Just remember my promises to you about how things are between us and always will be."

Now recalling the time when she had seen him materializing from that strange mist, Mia wondered if she would be seeing something similar again.

She squared her shoulders and tightened her jaw, for she would have to be strong. Was she going to discover that this man she loved with all of her heart was even more mystical than his Shaman grandfather?

No matter what happened, she could never love him less.

"I shall remember," Mia murmured, smiling at him, then hurrying outside the tepee.

They were soon at the longboat where the two trappers were sat, their eyes filled with terror.

Wolf Hawk helped Mia into the boat, to sit beside him. The trappers stayed where they were, facing her and Wolf Hawk.

Mia could see how shaken the men were as Wolf Hawk shoved the boat out into deeper water, then boarded it and grabbed up the paddle. Again he headed the boat toward the fort.

As they rounded a bend in the river, Mia gasped at what she saw. The earthquake had loosened the land all around the fort, and that whole section of shoreline was close to breaking away, which would take the fort with it.

She looked quickly to where she had buried her father. She sighed with relief to see that the grave lay untouched beneath the shade of the trees.

"Lord, oh, Lord, don't take us back to the fort," Jeb suddenly cried out, causing Wolf Hawk to glare at him. "The land is just barely clinging to the shore, and the fort is on that piece of ground that has loosened. Please don't take us there. Have mercy. Oh, please have mercy on our souls."

Wolf Hawk looked away from him and continued paddling toward the fort. When he reached that stretch of land that led to the gates of the fort, he beached the boat. He stepped from it and helped Mia to the ground.

Then he nodded at the trappers. "Come with me," he said hoarsely. "Now."

The men reluctantly walked toward the open gate of the fort.

Mia stepped aside when they reached the gate, and Wolf Hawk shoved them both inside.

Mia sheepishly followed. She grew pale when she saw where Wolf Hawk was taking the men. It was to a dark, dank cabin, where chains hung from the walls.

She knew this must have been where prisoners were once kept.

She saw how the two trappers cowered, then cried out in pain, as Wolf Hawk fastened them to the wall with the chains.

Suddenly a lone wolf entered the tiny space. The men cowered and grew even paler at the sight of the wolf pacing back and forth in front of them, its eyes never leaving them.

Even Mia was afraid, for she knew that the wolf could kill them in an instant. She tried to tell herself she was safe because she was with Wolf Hawk.

A moment later he stepped outside and let out a strange sort of howl, to call more wolves there. Goose bumps sprang up on Mia's flesh. She was stunned, yet she fought off her fear, for she knew that Wolf Hawk would never do anything to harm her.

Yet she trembled and stepped as far away from the men as possible when several more wolves appeared and entered the dungeonlike room. The beautiful animals ignored Mia, pacing back and forth in front of the two trembling trappers.

Another wolf came into the room and stopped at Mia's side. She swallowed hard and forced herself not to be afraid when that wolf suddenly transformed itself back into Wolf Hawk.

He turned to her. He saw the look of wonder in her eyes and was so glad there was no longer any fear there. She now knew his secret, and had found a way to accept it.

"It is time to go," he said. "All that must be done here, is done. The rest will take care of itself."

Mia slowly nodded, took his hand, then glanced over her shoulder at the men. They screamed and begged for mercy as the wolves got closer and closer to them.

Mia left the fort with Wolf Hawk, stopping just outside the walls.

"I shall wait while you spend a few moments with your father and then we must return home," Wolf Hawk said, taking her hand for a moment, then releasing it as she walked over to the mound of earth, and bent to her knees beside it.

"Papa, oh, Papa, I miss you so," she whispered. "And, Papa, I have so much to learn, but Wolf Hawk is eager to teach me."

She closed her eyes for a moment and recalled how moments ago the man she loved had been something besides a man . . . a powerfully muscled wolf who seemed to have control over those that had gone into the cabin to torment the evil men.

"I will be alright, Papa," she went on. "I could not have a better man to protect me than Wolf Hawk. I love him. He loves me. When I have our first child, I shall bring the baby here for you to know."

She could feel Wolf Hawk waiting for her, she herself wanted to leave this place of mystery as fast as she could. Once they returned to the village, surely all of this strangeness would be left behind. She had never seen Wolf Hawk be anything but his people's leader while she was at the village with him. She doubted that his people even knew the true powers that he held within his grip.

"I love you, Papa," Mia whispered, then rose to her feet and went to Wolf Hawk. "I'm ready."

She shivered when she again heard the two trappers screaming and shouting. They had been made to know the evil they did.

Mia would not think of what their final end might be.

All she knew was that the wolves were still there with the men. She believed that those wolves were the spirits of some of Wolf Hawk's warriors who had left this earth.

"Let us put this all behind us," Wolf Hawk said, lifting Mia into his powerful arms. "What you saw today was something that could have made you afraid to love me. I am glad that your faith in me and my love for you is so strong that you could accept what you saw. There is even more, my woman, that you will also learn about me, but for now, this is enough."

"Yes, enough," Mia murmured as he drew her lips against his and gave her a kiss filled with passion and heat.

"The moon is full," he whispered against her lips. "The river is calm. Let us go home, my woman, and make love."

"Yes, let's," she whispered, sucking in a wild gasp of pleasure when he reached a hand up inside the skirt of her dress, his fingers caressing her where she already ached for him.

"I love you so," Mia whispered against his lips. "I love everything about you. Everything."

That was all Wolf Hawk needed to hear.

Chapter Thirty-one

If ever wife was happy as a man,
Compare with me, ye women, if you can.
                                        —*Anne Bradstreet*

The morning sun was creeping up from the horizon, tinting the sky a soft pink as Mia awakened after her first full night of being Wolf Hawk's wife.

"You are awake," Wolf Hawk said. He moved closer to Mia amid their pelts and blankets beside the fire pit, where only cold ashes now lay.

The temperature outside had risen, so that no fires were built inside the tepees. All of the cooking was done outside by the women of the village. And the very bottom edges of all the tepees were rolled up and secured, allowing fresh, cool air to sweep through the opening.

Mia felt it even now, the sweetness of the morning air, which held the scent of cook fires already being built throughout the village.

"Yes, husband, I am awake," Mia said, turning to Wolf Hawk. "How could I not be? We forgot to cover Georgina last night and daylight awakened her. She is already singing."

"And a beautiful song it is," Wolf Hawk said, gazing over at Georgina, who was moving back

and forth on her perch as she continued to sere-
nade the two love birds.

Mia moved even closer to Wolf Hawk, whose
nakedness fired her senses. She felt somewhat
shameful because she always needed him.

But she loved him so much, and he loved her, it
was only natural for them to ache to make love
whenever they could.

And, ah, how wonderful it was for Mia to be
able to go to sleep in her husband's arms, as well
as wake up snuggled next to him.

"I love calling you husband," Mia murmured,
slowly running a hand down the smoothness of
his chest, then lower, past his flat stomach.

She giggled when her touch caused his manhood to jerk with pleasure beneath her fingers.

"And I love doing this to you," she murmured.

He reached out and swept her body against
his. Her hand now rested on his muscular but-
tocks.

"I love doing this," he said huskily, covering
her lips with his. Passion ignited quickly between
them.

Mia wrapped a leg over his, their bodies now
fused, as though they were one. She twined her
arms around his neck as he quickly and gently slid
her beneath him and rolled on top of her.

Their lips quivered with the passion building
between them.

Mia sucked in a wild breath of pleasure when
Wolf Hawk swiftly entered her. His manhood
seemed to swell in her tightness, the pressure

causing their pleasure to intensify as he began his thrusts.

He moved his lips downward and swept a tongue around one of her nipples, causing Mia to moan with a pleasure she'd never known was possible until she and Wolf Hawk had made love that first time.

And now she was the wife of this man who always seemed to know exactly where to touch her. His caresses made her go almost wild with pleasure.

She clung to him as he kissed her again, his body ever moving against hers, causing ecstasy to sweep through her.

Happiness bubbled from deep within her as his fingers moved tantalizingly over her breasts, making maddeningly designed circles over each of them.

His eyes glazed, drugged with desire, Wolf Hawk paused to gaze into Mia's eyes. He saw that they were hazy with her own building passion, while he, himself, felt the curl of heat growing in his lower body.

And then he kissed her again, his mouth smothering her outcry of ecstasy while he moved incessantly inside her, his own senses now reeling in drunken pleasure.

Her body a river of sensations, Mia twined her arms around Wolf Hawk's neck and rode with him in rhythmic ecstasy.

Wolf Hawk slid his lips from her mouth and breathed hard against the slight curve of her neck as he groaned out his pleasure. He made one last wild thrust inside her, knowing that she had found the same peak of pleasure as he. She was sighing and moaning, her eyes closed in the ultimate ecstasy.

And then their bodies became quiet, yet still together, as they both tried to catch their breath.

"I . . . I . . . have never felt such a wondrous joy as I just experienced. Ah, such a beautiful passion," Mia murmured, finally breathing softly.

Wolf Hawk rolled away from her and now lay beside her, his hand resting on her flat belly.

She turned to him and slowly ran her fingers through his thick, black hair, smoothing it away from his handsome face so that she would have full view of him.

She smiled at how this powerful chief's cheeks were flushed, and how she could see his pulse still beating hard in the vein in his neck. Clearly, he had received as much pleasure from what they had shared as she.

"And we have a lifetime ahead of us of the same," Wolf Hawk said.

He took her hand and guided it down to where he still throbbed from the intense pleasure that he had received from her body.

He closed his eyes and sucked in a wild breath of pleasure as she moved her hand on him. She now knew just how intensely or slowly to stroke him, to bring him alive again there and filled with need.

"You are very skilled, Lady Hawk, ah, so very skilled at what you do to your husband," Wolf

Hawk said, almost breathless now from the building rapture.

"Lady Hawk," Mia murmured, sighing. "I do love my Indian name. Thank you for giving it to me."

"My Lady Hawk," Wolf Hawk breathed out, then slid her beneath him and again gave her the pleasure that she begged of him.

And then they fell apart once more, each as flushed as the other.

"My energy is all gone now and the day is just beginning," Mia said, laughing softly. "I am not certain I can make you bread today, husband. Nor anything else, for that matter."

"What you just gave me is much more welcome than any bread," Wolf Hawk said, chuckling.

Then he sat up away from her. "And as for our meals today, would you like some fresh fish?" he asked.

He reached a hand out, gently took one of hers and drew her up to sit before him.

He gazed intensely into her eyes. "You told me once that what you enjoyed most about riding the river was fishing," he said.

"Yes, I did learn to love to fish. It always made my father so proud when I brought in a big catfish or trout," Mia murmured.

She recalled the last time she had fished with her father. The day before her mother's death she had brought in the largest catfish she had ever seen.

She would never forget the pride she had seen in her father's eyes as he held the fish out and measured its length with his eyes, then gave it back to her to prepare for their evening meal. She had proudly fileted it, and oh, how delicious it had been right out of her mother's frying pan!

"Why do you bring that up now?" Mia asked, raising her eyebrows. She laughed softly. "Are you wanting to have fish for our evening meal?"

"Only if you catch it for us," Wolf Hawk said, smiling as he saw Mia's eyes widen in wonder.

"You want me to . . . ?" she said, then laughed softly. "Of course you jest."

"No, there is no jesting about food in our lodge, Lady Hawk," Wolf Hawk said, rising. He reached down and grabbed her by the hand. "Come. Dress. A canoe awaits us, or would you rather go fishing in your Mia boat?"

"Mia boat?" Mia said.

"*Ho*, is not the longboat named after you?" Wolf Hawk said, now handing her a lovely doeskin dress that his cousin Little Snowbird had sewn for her to wear on outings with her husband, one that had no fancy designs of beads.

It was just a plain, fringed dress, but her husband had told her every dress looked beautiful on her, beaded, or not.

"Yes, it was named after me," Mia said, pulling the dress over her head, then reaching for her hairbrush.

Wolf Hawk quickly took the brush from her and turned her so that her back was to him. He began brushing her hair for her until it was freed of all tangles and lay shining over her shoulders and down her back.

He dropped the brush to the floor and turned her to face him. He framed her face between his hands, brought her lips to his, and sweetly kissed her.

"My wife," he whispered against her lips. "It is a wonder to me that you are now all mine. My Lady Hawk, my wife."

"Your wife," Mia said, her eyes taking in his handsomeness.

"Come, we will embarrass the warriors of my village when you, my wife, bring in a great catch of fish," Wolf Hawk said.

When they got outside, Mia was very aware that most of the women were already cooking over their fires and hers was not even lit yet.

She felt somewhat embarrassed about that. Surely the other women knew why her fire was not yet ready. They must have guessed what had delayed the newly married couple . . . that their chief and his wife were making love.

Mia blushed at that thought, squeezed Wolf Hawk's hand, and followed him to one of the canoes.

Inside the canoe Mia spotted fishing poles lying on the bottom and handmade lures.

She had always used worms or crickets when she fished rather than lures. She had enjoyed fishing even though it made her cringe when she placed a cricket on her hook. She loved hearing a cricket's song at night, especially now with Wolf

Hawk, when the stars were bright in the heavens and love was in the air.

At times, her new life seemed almost unreal. She could hardly believe that she had met such a wonderful man, someone who could care so much for her that he seemed actually to idolize her.

Well, she knew that he could not love her any more than she did him. He was everything to her. He was her world.

"Lady Hawk," Wolf Hawk said as he pulled the paddle rhythmically through the water. "In former times, my people used the *woca*, or spear, to fish. We would go out on the river at night, using torches of pine pitch to light our way. But today we fish by the sun's light, using special lures I have made."

Mia stiffened with excitement when she saw a fish suddenly flip from the water. She gasped, for it was the largest catfish she had ever seen, much larger than any she had ever caught before.

"Did you see it?" Mia squealed, picking up the fishing pole that was ready to use. Wolf Hawk had prepared it the day before.

"Steady," Wolf Hawk said, laying his paddle at the bottom of the canoe. He moved closer to Mia as she prepared to cast the line out into the water.

"Steady," Wolf Hawk said again, this time reaching out and actually steadying Mia's hand.

He watched with her for the catfish to make another leap. When it did, Wolf Hawk held his hand away from Mia as she flung the line out into the water near where they had seen the catfish.

"The catfish in this part of the river are huge," Wolf Hawk said, watching the water. "My people tell stories of them, and some of my warriors claim to have seen fish as big as a man."

"Truly?" Mia gasped, turning to gaze at Wolf Hawk in wonder.

Just as she said that, she felt a jerk on her line, and then a harder one. She gasped when the pole snapped in two and she watched the line moving quickly away in the water, with the fish at the other end.

Wolf Hawk suddenly dove into the water. He swam hard toward the line that was still being dragged through the water behind the fish, then grabbed it.

As he treaded water, he pulled on the line until finally the fish was in sight on the far end of it.

"There it is!" Mia squealed.

Wolf Hawk saw it, too, as it came closer and closer. Finally the fish was within touching distance.

He reached out, grabbed it, then holding it by the line, swam quickly back to the canoe and threw the fish into it. Mia clutched the line to stop the fish from flopping over the other side, into the water again.

She always avoided the eyes of the fish she caught, for she was so softhearted, she knew that if her eyes and the fish's eyes met, she would not have the heart to keep it out of the water any longer.

"Food is survival," Wolf Hawk said, pulling

himself into the canoe when he saw Mia's expression. "Do not ever feel guilty for having brought food to our lodge, be it fish, or deer. Be proud, especially today, the first day you are learning the ways of our people. This is only one lesson. There will be many more."

"I never want to disappoint you, so I will not let myself feel guilty at taking such a large fish from the water. Instead, I will feel very, very proud," Mia murmured.

She watched Wolf Hawk remove the line, then hold the fish out toward her again.

"Hold it and feel its weight," Wolf Hawk said. "I have never caught one so big, myself. Lady Hawk, you have made your husband very proud."

Mia beamed as she held the fish in her arms once again. But when she realized where the canoe had drifted, she turned pale.

She recognized this stretch of the river. Just around the bend was the old fort.

She and Wolf Hawk exchanged quick glances just as the canoe drifted past the bend.

"The . . . the . . . fort and the ground on which it was built are gone!" Mia gasped out, actually feeling the color drain from her face. "Gone!"

She looked quickly where she had last knelt beside her father's grave, and sighed with relief when she saw it was still there.

Then she looked at Wolf Hawk again. "How . . . ?" she murmured.

"The earthquake weakened the land, as you remember, and the tide must have finished the destruction," he said thickly. "It is now gone. All of it. And as my grandfather planned, the trappers have been removed from our land for always."

"The young braves shall now rest in peace," Mia murmured.

"*Ho*, in peace," Wolf Hawk said, reaching for one of her hands. "Let us go ashore so that you can speak to your father and tell him how happy you are in your new life. He will have cause to smile at you from the heavens."

"Yes, I would love that, and then I want to go home," Mia murmured. "Our home, husband. I want to cook you some fish!"

Wolf Hawk smiled at her, then took up the paddle and guided the canoe to shore.

He helped Mia from the boat and held her hand as he led her to the mound of earth. He stood with Mia as she gazed down at the grave. He could feel her pain as she spoke to her father, of how she missed him so much, and then her pride as she talked of her marriage and her happiness.

"Papa, I am now called Lady Hawk," she said, lifting her chin proudly as she gazed up at Wolf Hawk. "I never knew I could be so happy, Papa. But I am. Rest assured that I am."

Wolf Hawk placed his arm around her waist and drew her near to him.

He then took his turn speaking to her father.

"Your daughter, my Lady Hawk, will never want for a thing," he vowed. "I will see to her needs . . . all of them. She will be a happy woman. She is already as one with my people. She is beloved."

A soft breeze brushed across his cheek, and then Mia's.

They exchanged quick smiles, for they both felt her father's presence.

Mia now knew that he had heard, and he was happy for her.

Chapter Thirty-two

Though it was spring, snow could still be seen where trees shadowed the land. On a nearby hillside and across the meadows, flowers dotted the ground in a patchwork of color. Pussy willows were wearing their gray, fuzzy coats, and crocuses showed their bright faces of purple, white and yellow.

V-shaped flocks of birds flew high overhead, their squawking racket welcome since it had not been heard during the long months of winter.

It was the time of the spring hunt and Mia, who was now known by all as Lady Hawk, stood proud and very pregnant at the entranceway of hers and Wolf Hawk's tepee.

She was watching the warriors bringing in their heavy packs of beaver pelts, as well as many travois heavily laden with meat already cut into many portions.

Wolf Hawk led the way on his horse, pride in his smile as he found Mia standing there. He knew that she would be feeling guilty for not being able to join the other women as they met the warriors, ready to help unload what had been brought home from the successful hunt.

Mia was too heavy with child to join them, and the women understood.

Mia looked past Wolf Hawk, and saw their son of twelve winters. He sat proudly on his pony beside his father, returning from his very first hunt as a young brave.

His name was Spirit Hawk and he had been born in the exact image of his chieftain father, with the same intensely dark eyes, proud, lifted chin, and sculpted features.

Today he was attired as was his father, in a full fringed outfit, his coal black hair held back by a headband, then falling on down past his waist.

Spirit Hawk had skills with a bow and arrow that exceeded most his age, but not every youth had a father such as Wolf Hawk for a teacher.

Mia was so proud of the way Wolf Hawk spent so much time with both his children. Already, he was teaching Spirit Hawk the mystical secrets of his father and grandfather.

It did not worry Mia that her son might one day soar in the heavens as a hawk, or run on all fours as a beautiful, sleek wolf. She had grown used to her husband's secrets, and saw nothing wrong in her son walking in the same moccasins as his father and grandfather.

Talking Bird was now far past his hundredth winter and still did his magic whenever it was needed. Mia loved going and sitting and talking with the old Shaman, as did her two children.

Yes, there was more than a son to brag about. There was a daughter whose name was Recosha. She was now ten winters of age, and anxiously awaiting the birth of Mia's third child.

Recosha wanted a sister.

Mia cared not whether she had a boy or a girl this time; she was just so proud that she was giving her husband another child. She had never seen anyone who loved children more than Wolf Hawk, except for herself.

They made quite a pair, thinking so much alike about everything. It had been their destiny to meet. Their marriage was filled with love and devotion, and . . . happiness.

Thus far the white government had not interfered in the Bird Clan's lives. Wolf Hawk had made certain his people did nothing to warrant attention that might bring the white pony soldiers to their village.

No one had seemed to have missed the two trappers who had disappeared with the old fort after the earthquake.

As for Tiny? He, too, had never been seen again.

Mia had often wondered about him, whether or not he lived or died, after having lost one of his shoes, his deck of cards, and several strands of his hair. It was as though Tiny had just disappeared into thin air, and Mia only now and then wondered about him.

She frequented her father's grave, and often

wished that she could go back to where her mother had been buried. Unfortunately, she knew it was unlikely she would ever find that grave again. It had been quickly dug, and her mother quickly buried, for at that time she and her father had felt like targets of the lone Indian who had killed her mother.

Mia brushed all of her troubled thoughts aside as Wolf Hawk rode up in front of the tepee and dismounted.

She rushed outside and flung herself into his arms. "It is good to have you home again," she murmured. "And I saw the pride on your face when you looked at Spirit Hawk. I assume that means his hunt was good?"

"Very," Wolf Hawk said, now stepping away from Mia and watching, along with her, as Spirit Hawk dismounted from his pony and began helping unload the travois.

Recosha rushed up and stood beside Spirit Hawk, helping to hand out the portions of meat as each woman came for her share.

"And ah, what a pretty daughter we have," Wolf Hawk said.

Recosha resembled her mother, with her pale skin and green eyes, but her hair was very different from Mia's. It was coal black, thick, and worn in one long braid down her back. She was dressed in doeskin, the dress embellished with beautiful beads. Her moccasins reached up to her knees and were of doeskin, too, and also beaded.

"She is pretty, isn't she?" Mia said, smiling at Wolf Hawk. "We are so fortunate."

Wolf Hawk turned to her and gently placed a hand on her round belly. "We are very fortunate," he said, his eyes smiling into Mia's. He laughed softly. "I feel her moving in your belly. I do not think she is going to be as delicate as our Recosha."

"And you still assume that the third child will be a girl?" Mia said, giggling softly as she, too, felt the movement of her child inside her belly.

"Recosha wants a sister, and I believe she will get her wish," Wolf Hawk said, turning slow eyes back to Recosha.

Mia smiled inwardly, for she, too, believed she was going to have a daughter. Her husband had powers to make things happen as he wanted them to happen. If he said that he would soon father another daughter, then that was what the child would be.

As Wolf Hawk drew his hand away from Mia's belly, she placed her own there and felt such joy.

Wolf Hawk was her soul mate, the very air she breathed, and she knew they would be together for eternity.

She sighed as she thought to herself, *Could anything be more perfect?*

Dear Reader,

I hope you enjoyed reading *Savage Abandon*. The next book in my Savage series, which I am writing exclusively for Leisure books, is *Savage Sun*. This book is filled with much romance, excitement and a few surprises.

Those of you who are collecting my Indian romance novels, and want to hear more about the series and my entire backlist of Indian books, can send for my latest newsletter, autographed bookmark, and fan club information, by writing to:

Cassie Edwards
6709 N. Country Club Road
Mattoon, IL 61938

For a response, please include a self-addressed, stamped legal-sized envelope with your letter. Thank you for your support of my Indian series. I love writing about our nation's beloved Native Americans, our country's true first people.

Always,
Cassie Edwards